MEET THE

Fortune of th ~~ane Whitfield~~

Age: 33

Vital statistics: We're not sure which is sexier—his charming British accent, his brilliant mind or those eyes!

Claim to fame: He's a world-renowned architect whose genius is exceeded only by his popularity with women. He is also the illegitimate son of philandering millionaire Gerald Robinson, formerly known as Jerome Fortune.

Romantic prospects: It's *Keaton Whitfield.*

"The one thing you need to know about me is I'm nothing like my so-called father. The media may paint me as a heartbreaker, but it's not true. I have never made a promise I couldn't keep. In fact, I've decided to avoid women entirely while I'm here in Austin. Francesca Harriman doesn't count. She's my favorite waitress at Lola May's Homestyle Restaurant, and besides, everyone says she doesn't date. So there's no danger here. No possibility of falling for her golden curls, that creamy skin, that curvy figure... I simply love puzzles, and Francesca is an intriguing one. Why *doesn't* she date? And is there any man who could make her change her mind? Oh, wait. Right. I am avoiding women entirely..."

THE FORTUNES OF TEXAS:
The Secret Fortunes—
A new generation of heroes and heartbreakers!

Dear Reader,

I'm excited to welcome you back to life with the Fortunes of Texas. There are new adventures and discoveries and many more happy-ever-afters. Much like my heroine, Francesca Harriman, I wasn't the type of girl to be swept off my feet by a man. But if I had the opportunity, Keaton Fortune Whitfield is exactly the type of man I'd choose. He's handsome, kind and has the most amazing British accent.

Raised by a single mother, Keaton never expected to become a Fortune, and he has mixed feelings about Gerald Robinson, the man who broke his mom's heart. But when he meets Francesca, there's no questioning his feelings for her. There's an immediate spark of attraction between them that quickly turns into something far deeper.

Francesca has been burned by love in the past, so she's reluctant to believe that a handsome, sexy Fortune could want a regular girl like her. Can Keaton prove to this spunky waitress that he's the man to sweep her off her feet and make all her dreams come true?

Thank you for sharing their journey with me!

All the best,

Michelle Major

A Fortune
in Waiting

Michelle Major

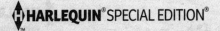
HARLEQUIN® SPECIAL EDITION®

Special thanks and acknowledgment are given to Michelle Major for her contribution to The Fortunes of Texas: The Secret Fortunes continuity.

Recycling programs
for this product may
not exist in your area.

ISBN-13: 978-0-373-62320-4

A Fortune in Waiting

Copyright © 2016 by Harlequin Books S.A.

Printed in U.S.A.

™ www.Harlequin.com

Michelle Major grew up in Ohio but dreamed of living in the mountains. Soon after graduating with a degree in journalism, she pointed her car west and settled in Colorado. Her life and house are filled with one great husband, two beautiful kids, a few furry pets and several well-behaved reptiles. She's grateful to have found her passion writing stories with happy endings. Michelle loves to hear from her readers at michellemajor.com.

Books by Michelle Major

Harlequin Special Edition

Crimson, Colorado

Christmas on Crimson Mountain
Always the Best Man
A Baby and a Betrothal
A Very Crimson Christmas
Suddenly a Father
A Second Chance on Crimson Ranch
A Kiss on Crimson Ranch

A Brevia Beginning
Her Accidental Engagement
Still the One

The Fortunes of Texas: All Fortune's Children

Fortune's Special Delivery

The Fortunes of Texas: Cowboy Country

The Taming of Delaney Fortune

Visit the Author Profile page
at Harlequin.com for more titles.

To Susan and Marcia for everything you do
to make this journey such an enjoyable one.

Prologue

Keaton Whitfield watched the snow fall outside the front window of his mother's cozy flat on the edge of London. The fluffy flakes, cast in a golden hue thanks to the streetlight, floated down for only a few minutes before the night sky cleared again.

"I can't remember the last time it snowed on Christmas," his mother said, coming to stand beside him. "It's good luck."

Keaton wrapped an arm around his mum, pulling her in for a quick hug. She was several inches shorter than his own six foot two and her dark hair was liberally streaked with gray, but she still had the same comforting scent of lavender that he always associated with her. "Everything is good luck to you." He dropped a kiss on the top of her head.

"You are my best bit of luck," she answered and

turned to face him. "I'm so glad you chose to spend Christmas with us this year, Keaton."

"I wouldn't want to be anywhere else, Mum." He thought for a moment of his own empty flat across town. It had been almost two years since he'd headed up the renovation of the building he lived in near the center of the city. His apartment was spacious and new, boasting a state-of-the-art design that had led one London magazine to name Keaton the heir apparent to one of the UK's most famous architects, Lord Foster.

But as much as Keaton appreciated the style and amenities of his posh apartment, he'd spent each of the past thirty-three holidays with his mother, having Christmas dinner around the slightly shabby oak table in the house where he'd been raised. Keaton might have earned the finer things in life through his success, but he'd always appreciate where he came from and the woman who sacrificed so much to make sure he had a good life.

"Yet you're still set on leaving me?" she asked, a small catch to her voice.

He turned and glanced down, hating the worry his mother couldn't quite hide from her gentle blue eyes. Anita Whitfield still wore her hair in the same simple bob she'd had since Keaton was a lad. Delicate lines fanned out from the corners of her eyes, and her mouth pulled down on either side before she forced it into a smile.

"I'm moving to Austin for a project," he corrected. "That isn't the same thing as leaving you. I'll be gone for a few months and now that you have a smartphone, we can text or FaceTime whenever you want."

"That phone you gave me is so smart it makes me feel like a regular idiot," she complained, making Keaton smile.

"You're getting the hang of it," he told her.

She sniffed. "In the past few days, I've made more accidental calls with my bottom than by actually dialing any numbers."

He pulled his mother in for a hug. "I'm going to miss you."

She squeezed him tightly before stepping away. "I hope you know you don't have anything to prove to your father," she whispered.

"Gerald Robinson," Keaton said through clenched teeth, "is not my father."

"Keaton." Anita cupped his cheek like she used to do when he was a boy. "I know he hurt you."

He turned toward the display of his mother's Lemax Christmas Village. He rearranged the tiny figures in front of Santa's workshop, setting them together in groups of three or four. As a boy, his mother's miniature buildings, figurines and holiday landscapes had been off limits, but he'd routinely snuck over to it, setting the small porcelain figurines into family units, the kind he'd never known.

Until last year, the identity of the man who had deserted his mother when she'd been pregnant with Keaton had remained a mystery. Keaton had been aware, in the inexplicable way of children, that his mother's heart had been broken by her short-lived love affair. Even as boy, he'd hated the wistful sorrow that filled her eyes when he'd asked about his father. So he'd stopped asking. Instead, he'd channeled his energy into hating the stranger who—to his young mind—was the reason his mum had been forced to work two jobs and still continually scrimp and save in order to support the two of them.

Now that he knew that man was Gerald Robinson, the ridiculously successful and wealthy technology mogul, he was more determined than ever to prove that he'd been better off never knowing his father as a boy.

"You were the one he hurt," he answered. "Gerald Robinson is nothing to me. I don't have a thing to prove to that man."

He said the words with conviction, even though he and his mother both knew they were a lie.

Anita placed a hand on his arm, squeezing softly. "You'll do well in America," she murmured, "and I know it will be lovely to visit with the other Fortunes again."

Keaton nodded. As bitter of a pill as it was to learn that Gerald, who had years ago faked his death as Jerome Fortune so that he could start a new life, was his biological father, Keaton had enjoyed getting to know his half brothers and sisters. He'd always envied his mates who came from big families, and being a part of the Fortune clan—despite his feelings for Gerald— filled a bit of the void inside him.

"You two lovelies had better get seated," a voice called from the hallway that led to the flat's kitchen, "Or you're going to miss the whole of the Christmas feast."

Keaton took a breath and smiled, watching his mother do the same. Lydia Miles, one of Anita's close-knit circle of friends, beckoned to them.

Keaton might not have had a large family growing up, but he'd never lacked for love. His mother had cultivated a group of women, her own little village of mother hens, and Keaton had been at the center of their sweetly smothering love and attention.

As he followed his mother into the kitchen, he was accosted on all sides by this brigade of pseudo-mums. They kissed and hugged and pinched his cheek as if, at six foot two, he didn't tower above the lot of them.

"I've made your favorite pudding," Mary Jane told him.

"And I've brought prawns," Lydia added.

Not to be outdone, Jessa held a plate under his nose. "Don't forget my pigs in a blanket."

Keaton laughed and plucked one of the bacon-wrapped sausages off the tray. "I'm going to need to loosen my belt a notch after this dinner," he said and popped it into his mouth.

"Ah, dearie," Lydia said, patting him on the shoulder. "Word on the street is you have plenty of notches to go around."

Keaton promptly choked on the sausage, and the women gathered even closer to take turns gently slapping him on the back.

"Give him some room," Anita shouted with a laugh. The other women backed away and his real mother handed him a glass of water.

"There are no notches on my belt," he muttered, clearing his throat.

His mother raised a brow.

"At least not recently," he amended.

Ever since discovering that Gerald might have a whole passel of illegitimate Fortunes from various dalliances with women over the years, Keaton had curbed his own dating life until it was nonexistent. He was careful with women—both their hearts and in the bedroom—and had remained friends with almost all of his ex-girlfriends. But he still wanted there to be no mistaking the fact that he was nothing like his womanizing father.

Part of why he'd taken the position with the firm in Austin was to work with his half brother Ben on tracking down other children sired by Gerald. Keaton was determined to make it clear that he hadn't inherited the "ship in every port" tendency of the elder Robinson.

"Sit down," his mother said, pushing him into a chair at the head of the table. "We can talk about your plans to settle down while we eat."

"I have no plans to settle down," he argued, earning a round of reprimanding tsks from the other women. "Sorry, ladies." He grabbed the wineglass that sat to one side of his plate and took a fortifying gulp. "I'm focused on work right now."

"Work doesn't warm you under the covers on a cold winter night," Lydia mused.

"And you're such a lovely chap." Mary Jane beamed at him.

Jessa nodded. "A true catch, Keaton. That's what you are. And those of us who love and adore you aren't getting any younger."

Although he had a feeling he'd regret it, he asked, "Why would you need to get younger?"

His mother dropped into the chair next to him and took his hand. "We love you, darling. But we want some grandbabies to spoil."

Keaton stifled a groan and took another drink, hoping his mother had more than one bottle on the ready. This was going to be the longest Christmas night of his life.

Chapter One

"Y'all back away from that poor man or else his supper's liable to get cold."

The two waitresses who had been leaning over the counter at Lola May's Homestyle Restaurant slowly straightened.

"Just say one more thing for us," Emmalyn, the petite blonde, cooed.

"How about 'I'll have mine shaken not stirred,'" prompted the buxom redhead, whose nametag read "Brandi, with an *i*"—as if customers in Texas needed the clarification.

"I mean it, you two. Get going." Lola May, owner and namesake of the diner, swatted at the two young women with the corner of a dishtowel.

"Another time, luv," Keaton told Brandi, earning a girlish giggle as she backed away.

Lola May, who looked every bit of her sixty-plus years but had a mischievous smile that softened her hard edges, rolled her blue eyes at him. She was exactly the image he had of the type of woman who would run a casual, neighborhood diner in Austin, Texas. One part old-school cowgirl mixed with two parts aging hippie.

Her platinum blond hair, with about a half inch of gray roots, was spiked around her pixie face and each of the past three days he'd been in for dinner, her heavy eye makeup had matched her sparkling earrings. The color du jour was turquoise green and it gave her clear blue eyes an almost otherworldly look when she blinked. The lines across her forehead and fanning out from her eyes could only have been put there by years of stress and hard work.

He recognized them because they reminded him of his mother. Although Anita and Lola May on the surface had nothing in common, there was something about the diner owner that helped ease the twinges of loneliness he'd felt since arriving in Austin a week ago.

The diner was directly across the street from the site of the project he'd come to America to manage, and only a few blocks from the apartment he'd rented. It had been easy to slip into the pattern of having dinner each night at Lola May's lime-green Formica counter.

He forced his gaze not to stray to the woman hunched over a laptop in the corner booth. That particular waitress had nothing to do with the reason he'd so quickly become a diner regular. Or so he'd been trying to convince himself for the past week.

Lola May wagged a red-tipped nail in his direction.

"You'll never get any peace if you keep charming the waitresses with that accent and your cheeky smile."

Keaton winked at the older woman. "Well, darlin'," he drawled in an exaggerated Texas accent, "would it make you happy if I sounded more like a local?"

"Stick to 007," she said, barking out a laugh. "'Cause you sure ain't no John Wayne."

He bit back a grin when she slid a plate with a piece of apple pie onto the counter in front of him. "I don't remember ordering that," he argued half-heartedly.

"But you're going to devour it as always," she shot back then leaned closer. "You've ended every meal here with a slice of my pie. Trust Miss Lola May, handsome. I know what you need."

At the word *need*, Keaton couldn't help glance to the corner booth.

"Need and want are two different things, sugar," Lola May said softly.

"Everyone flirts with me except her."

Keaton didn't realize he'd spoken the words out loud until Lola May chuckled. "Don't get your knickers in a twist over Francesca," she cautioned. "It isn't that she doesn't like you, but our girl gives new meaning to the phrase 'nose to the grindstone.'"

One side of Keaton's mouth curved as he watched the gorgeous blonde in the corner blow a wayward curl out of her face before typing furiously on her laptop's keyboard.

Francesca. He'd heard the other waitresses call her that, and the name fit her. With her mass of golden hair, creamy skin and her lushly curved figure, Francesca looked more like a Botticelli muse than a waitress in a diner near Austin's trendy South Congress neighborhood.

"She's taking a full course load over at the university," Lola May continued, "in addition to her schedule here. I don't think she's had a day—or even an hour—off in months."

"Why does she take on so much?"

"That's her story, handsome." Lola May picked up his empty dinner plate and pushed the pie closer to him. "I'll just tell you she's a great little gal and deserves better than what—" She paused until Keaton glanced up at her then continued, "Or *who* she got stuck with in her life."

Keaton watched as Francesca moved a hand to the back of her neck and rubbed the muscles there. Well, if she needed a massage, he'd be glad to...

No.

An image of Gerald Robinson popped into his mind and he willed it away. He'd committed to a moratorium on dating during his time in Austin. It seemed easier to go cold turkey on the dating front than to have temptation constantly beckoning to him. He wasn't going to take the chance that anyone, especially his new siblings, might confuse him with the man who'd broken his mother's heart so many years ago.

Still, he couldn't seem to look away from the blonde. Just as Lola May disappeared into the kitchen, Francesca's head lifted. Her eyes widened as their gazes clashed and sparks seemed to dance on the air between them.

Keaton swallowed, his mouth suddenly dry as his body went on alert in a way that was wholly unfamiliar. He liked women. He appreciated women. Hell, he'd been raised solely by women. He'd had plenty of girl-friends and recognized mutual attraction.

Yet there was something different about this Francesca, and damn if he didn't want to figure out what it was. He'd loved puzzles as a kid. Alone in the flat after school with his mum at work, he'd spent hours poring over jigsaw pieces, trying to decipher exactly where they fit to make the picture complete.

That's what Francesca… Bloody hell, he didn't even know her last name. But that's what she felt like to him. A missing piece. Maybe he'd spent too long in his own company, but he knew he'd have a difficult time walking away until he understood exactly where she fit in his life.

He had a feeling the trick was going to be convincing her to let him.

Francesca Harriman slammed shut the door of her apartment above the diner and toed off one of the well-worn cowboy boots she'd been wearing all day, kicking it across the floor.

It landed with a thud against the coffee table, and a moment later, her roommate, Ciara James, burst from the bathroom. She was clutching a towel around her, water dripping from her long dark hair, and brandishing a…

"Is that the toilet bowel scrubber?" Francesca took a step back.

Ciara blew out a relieved breath and lowered the makeshift weapon. "You scared the pants off me," she said with a laugh.

"You were in the shower," Francesca countered and

kicked off her other boot. "I doubt you were wearing pants."

"Give me thirty seconds before you melt down," Ciara answered, pointing the toilet bowl brush at Francesca. She disappeared back into the bathroom and Francesca dropped to the sofa, letting her head fall back onto the cushions.

She closed her eyes and concentrated on moving air in and out of her lungs at a normal rate. She wasn't going to melt down. She did not have time for a major freak out, or even one of the minor variety.

So why wouldn't her stupid heartbeat settle? The answer that appeared in her brain was in the form of pair of sinfully sexy blue eyes staring at her from across the diner.

With a growl, she jumped up from the couch and stalked to the postage-stamp-sized galley kitchen. She stood on tiptoe and reached for the top shelf of the cabinet, sighing slightly as her fingers closed around the bar of chocolate Ciara had stashed there.

"Hey," her roommate shouted and Francesca whirled around, tearing off the wrapper and shoving a bite of blessedly rich chocolate into her mouth. "That's my secret spot," Ciara complained. "It's hidden from you."

"You've got to do better than that," Francesca said after chewing. "I'm a professional chocolate hound."

"Girl, you need more willpower."

"I've got an accounting exam the day after tomorrow," Francesca said with a groan. "I need brain food."

"I left you two squares on the table this morning," Ciara answered, "just like you told me to do."

Francesca sagged against the counter and handed

over the remainder of the chocolate bar. "I know. I'm weak. I'm so weak."

With a small laugh, Ciara broke off another two squares and handed them to Francesca. "I have a feeling the emergency is related to more than your classes, but desperate times and all that."

"You're a life saver, Ci."

"Do you want to talk about why you came slamming in here like someone had just stolen your favorite bottle of conditioner?"

Francesca smiled. "If you had these curls to tame," she said, pulling at the ends of her hair, "you'd take your conditioning seriously, too." She nibbled the corner of a chocolate square—a nibble full of willpower and self-control. "It's the Brit," she whispered after a moment.

Her friend blinked before a wide grin spread across her face. "The one who's been eating at the diner every day this week?"

"I need to concentrate," Francesca answered with a nod. "I can't with him lurking around Lola May's all the time. He's distracting."

"In the best way possible," Ciara agreed. "And I wouldn't exactly call ordering food and leaving awesome tips 'lurking.'"

"He's a good tipper?"

"Amazing. A fact that you would know if you didn't trade tables every time he sat in your section."

"I don't… It isn't… He makes me nervous."

"It's the way he looks at you."

"He doesn't *look* at me in any way," Francesca argued, biting down on her lip. "It's the accent. It's weird."

Ciara shook her head. "Weird is Mr. Fenke spooning his leftovers into all those little plastic bags he carries in his pockets. The accent is hot." She leaned in closer. "The way he looks at you is even hotter, like he wants to carry you across the moors in the misty morning fog."

"There are no moors in Austin."

"You know what I mean."

Francesca did know, and that was the problem. Keaton Whitfield—yes, she'd researched his name from one of the receipts in the register—made her wish they lived in a land of romantic moors and mist and that she was the type of woman to be carried anywhere by a man.

More like the type to carry his bags.

"I'm finally getting caught up on life," she told Ciara. "I can't afford to backslide again."

"Not every man is going to treat you like your ex-boyfriend. Lou the Louse was a special kind of jerk."

"I get that." Bitterness welled up in Francesca at the mention of his name. She'd dated Louis Rather for almost six years, and the fact that she'd been stupid enough to think he loved her still made her mad enough to spit. She'd put her entire life on hold to cater to a man, and when she'd finally left him, it was with the bone-deep conviction that she'd never make that same mistake again. "I was a fool for Lou for way too long. I don't trust myself to recognize heartbreak when it's standing right in front of me."

"Whoa, there, cowgirl." Ciara's smile was gentle. "You've just skipped over all the fun parts and gone straight to heartbreak."

"That's where I end up with men," Francesca muttered.

Ciara sighed. "I heard the hottie Brit say he was only in town for a few months. He's some kind of bigwig architect working on the Austin Commons project." She boosted herself up onto the counter. "Think of it as short-term fun."

"That's not exactly how my mind or my heart works."

"Come on, Francesca. You work and study all the time. You never go out. You don't date. You're only twenty-four, and you are the least fun person I know."

"I'm fun," Francesca protested, crossing her arms over her chest. "I'm a ton of fun."

"Prove it." Ciara pointed a finger in Francesca's direction. "Flirt with the Brit."

Chapter Two

The following evening, Francesca untied her apron and hung it on a peg in the back hallway of Lola May's, taking an extra moment to smack her open palm against the wall a few times.

Since her conversation with Ciara, she'd thought of little else besides flirting with Keaton. The problem was Francesca didn't know how to flirt. She'd only had one boyfriend in her life, and she and Lou had started dating back when they were still in high school. He was the bad boy of their class, an indie rocker who wore leather and a permanent scowl. All the girls from her tight-knit Austin community had crushed on him, including Francesca, even though she could barely bring herself to make eye contact.

But Lou had chosen her, literally picked her out of the crowd during one of his concerts at a neighborhood festival. After that, they were a couple. No flirting needed. She belonged to him.

At first she'd been overwhelmed and embarrassingly grateful. For a girl who'd grown up with the nicknames "Fat Frannie" and "Frizzy Frannie," gaining the attention of a boy like Lou had felt accomplishment enough. There was no doubt in either of their minds that Lou was doing her a great favor by letting her be his girlfriend.

For years, Francesca had shown her gratitude by taking care of him and his bandmates, which had left her more of a glorified roadie than a girlfriend. It sure hadn't left her much inclination or opportunity for flirting, unless it was vicariously as she watched a parade of groupies throwing themselves at Lou. Apparently, that kind of overt flirting worked with some men because she'd eventually found Lou in the arms of one of those same groupies.

So, yeah, Francesca had never had much use for flirting. Her skills at talking to men weren't just rusty. They were non-existent, especially when the man was as handsome as Keaton. Emmalyn and Brandi, the other two waitresses who had shared yesterday's shift with her, had no such problems.

Maybe Ciara had imagined the way he'd looked at Francesca. What did either of them know about how things were done in England, anyway? Chances were he gave that smoldering, carry-you-off-across-the-moors look to every woman.

She pulled her laptop bag off the hook and headed down to her corner booth. The booth didn't exactly belong to her, but as long as the restaurant wasn't full, Lola May let her use it to study. Francesca was such a fixture in the corner that the diner's regulars purposely left that table empty.

Just as she walked out, she heard a deep voice boom, "We don't need no fancy-schmantzy strip mall clogging up the street, and we don't need no foreigner trying to tell us how things should be built in Texas."

Francesca suppressed a groan and searched for Lola May in the restaurant. Johnny Keller was one of her least favorite customers. A long-time resident of the neighborhood, he was loud and brash and the stingiest tipper she'd ever met.

She knew his opinion about the recent gentrification of the neighborhood, including the project Keaton was developing. Everyone in a ten-block radius knew Johnny's opinion and it was always negative. Lola May could keep him in line, but Francesca didn't see her feisty boss at the moment. Then she remembered Lola May had taken off early to go watch her grandson's Little League game. No wonder Johnny had picked tonight to give grief to Keaton.

She couldn't quite make out Keaton's quiet response, but from the way Johnny's shoulders stiffened, it wasn't what the old blowhard wanted to hear.

"I'm not sure if you're aware of this, boy," Johnny was saying now, "but our people won the war against your people. Take that as hint, ya hear?"

"Are you referring to the Revolutionary War?" Keaton inclined his head. "The one that was fought over two hundred years ago?"

Johnny placed his meaty hands on his hips. "Texas never forgets."

Francesca stepped between the two men before Keaton could answer. "Johnny, Texas wasn't even a state at that time." She made her voice light and teasing. No use antagonizing him. "You know we would have been the capital of the whole dang country if we'd been around back then."

She darted a glance at Keaton, who looked like he was trying to hold back a smile, then forced her gaze to return to Johnny. If Keaton smiled at her she'd probably melt into a puddle all over the floor. This was the closest she'd been to him and the proximity made little sparks dance all over her skin.

"Damn straight, honey," Johnny agreed. "You don't mess with Texas."

She put a gentle hand on his arm. "And there's no need to mess with a man who's just doing his job."

Johnny shook his head. "I'm telling you, we don't need more highfalutin types changing up the spirit of the area."

"I wouldn't let Lola May hear you say that," Francesca warned, dropping her voice to a conspiratorial whisper.

"Why?" Johnny leaned closer. The man had a healthy fear of the diner's hot-tempered owner. "Don't tell me she supports all this new stuff."

"She's keeping an open mind," Francesca said, giving a small shrug. "We all need to, Johnny. I've lived here my whole life, but change is bound to come and it doesn't have to be bad." She nodded toward Keaton without making eye contact. "He may be British, but he's got a fantastic reputation as an architect. Our neighborhood is in good hands with Keaton Whitfield."

She held her breath as Johnny looked between her and Keaton. Other than the fact that he liked to hear himself talk, the man was basically harmless. But Francesca needed to get to her review sheet for accounting, so she didn't want to prolong this conversation. Plus, she could feel Keaton's gaze on her almost as if it were a physical touch. The man was seriously messing with her equilibrium.

"If you're vouching for him, Miss Frannie, then I guess I'll give him a chance." He shoved a hand past her and Keaton shook it. "I'll be keeping my eyes on you and your fancy complex."

"Of that I have no doubt," Keaton answered, each word clipped.

"Great." Francesca blew out a quick breath. "Brandi," she called. "I'd like to buy these two fine gentlemen a piece of pie."

Johnny flashed a broad grin while Keaton held up a hand. "Generous," he murmured, "but not—"

The other man clapped him hard on the back. "Boy, if a beautiful woman offers you pie, don't say no."

"Pecan for Johnny," Francesca continued, "and apple for our friend from across the pond."

"Got it," Brandi shouted.

"Enjoy, fellas," Francesca said quickly, still avoiding Keaton's blue gaze. She hurried to the safety of her corner booth and slid in with a sigh. Crisis avoided—both Johnny making a bigger scene and her revealing what a bumbling idiot she was around Keaton.

It didn't take long to become engrossed in her studies. Accounting was her toughest subject and the more she looked at the numbers, the more of a jumble they became in her head. She was staring at a particularly challenging problem when she felt someone approach the booth.

By the way butterflies zipped across her stomach, she didn't even need to look up to know who it was.

"May I join you?" Keaton asked in his rich accent.

The thoughtfulness of that question made a soft warmth spread through her. Most people at the diner just plopped down when they needed something, as if Francesca's opinion on whether she wanted company didn't matter.

She appreciated having her opinion matter to someone, even in such an insubstantial decision.

"Or not," Keaton continued. "I can see you're busy. Perhaps another time."

When he started to walk away, his mouth pressed into a thin line, she realized she hadn't actually given him an answer.

Add rude to her list along with bumbling and idiot.

"Please sit down," she called to him.

He turned and slipped into the seat across from her.

"How was the pie?" she asked, her words sounding embarrassingly breathless.

"Worth enduring Johnny's company while I ate it," he said with a half smile. "Thank you for that and for diffusing the situation. You are the prettiest knight in shining armor I've ever met."

She was so busy watching to see if the half smile turned into a full grin that it took a minute for his words to sink in. Had he just called her pretty?

"How did you know I prefer apple?"

She shrugged. "Lola May's isn't huge. You order a slice of apple pie every night."

"It's the best." He leaned a little closer. "You also know my name."

"The diner caters to regulars. You're becoming a regular, Keaton, so I know your name."

"I appreciate that, Francesca," he answered.

Lord have mercy, it was a good thing she was sitting down because the way her name sounded in his rich, cultured voice made her knees go weak.

"You know I'm an architect."

She felt color rise to her cheeks but didn't bother to deny it. "Yes."

"And the bit about my reputation?"

She huffed out a soft laugh. "I guessed at that."

One of his thick brows rose.

"Someone is sinking a ton of money into the Austin Commons project across the street. Reports say it's going to be the new retail and residential anchor for the neighborhood. They wouldn't leave the design to someone who couldn't handle it." Now she leaned in, something about the warmth in his gaze inviting her closer. "Was I wrong about you?"

"No."

"Are you famous?"

The smile widened. "In some circles, I suppose."

"I also heard," she murmured, "that you're part of the Fortune family."

He nodded, his blue eyes turning cool as he sat back against the vinyl-covered cushion of the booth. Interesting. Most people she knew would be shouting their connection to such a powerful family from the rooftops. Keaton seemed uncomfortable that she'd mentioned it. All traces of the smile disappeared from his face, making him look no less handsome but a lot more intimidating.

"It was pretty big news in Austin when Gerald Rob-

inson was revealed to be that Fortune heir who everyone thought was dead."

"Jerome Fortune."

"Right," she agreed. "Gerald Robinson is really Jerome Fortune. He's your father?"

"He is."

"Is that why you took on Austin Commons? To get
to know your dad?"

"No," he answered, the word spoken through
clenched teeth. "I want nothing to do with the man, although I'm happy to spend time with my half siblings."

It seemed she'd struck a nerve, so she quickly
changed the subject. "I always wanted brothers and
sisters." She reached for her water glass and took a
long drink, suddenly aware that she was sitting in Lola
May's, having a conversation with Keaton Fortune
Whitfield. So much for all her plans about flirting.

She was lucky to be able to put a complete sentence
together with him watching her from those gorgeous
blue eyes. The lashes that surrounded them were so
long they looked almost unreal. The strong line of his
jaw and the faint shadow of stubble covering it bal-
anced his beautiful eyes and full mouth.

"You're an only child?" he prompted, the half smile
returning, as if he could read her mind and understood
exactly his effect on her.

She nodded. "It was just my mom and me."

"I was raised by a single mum, as well." He blew
out a breath. "The whole time I was growing up, she
worked at least two jobs to support me. She was my
hero."

All she could do was stare at him. Of all the things
this man could have said, there was nothing more en-

dearing to Francesca than how much he obviously loved his mother.

He flashed a full-fledged grin, somewhat self-deprecating, as if he hadn't meant to share that detail with her. "Do I sound like a mummy's boy?"

"Hardly," she said on a small laugh. "You sound like the type of son every mother dreams about." She paused then said, "I like the way you say 'mum' with your accent."

"This coming from the woman with the adorable twang."

"I'm a proud Texan native," she told him, hitching a thumb at herself. "Go Longhorns. Keep Austin weird."

"Remember the Alamo," he added.

She giggled. "Exactly."

"What are you studying?" He tapped a finger on the pile of notes in front of her.

"Accounting," she said with a sigh. "I have a test tomorrow and it took everything I had to pull out an A last semester. This class is going to kill me."

"Not going for a finance degree, I take it?"

"I'm a business major with a concentration in marketing. It's not that I don't like accounting…"

He nodded. "Because most people find it fascinating."

She laughed again. For all her nerves around Keaton, it was also surprisingly easy to laugh with him. It had been a long time since Francesca had joked around with a man, other than her customers at the diner.

"I'm not sure *fascinating* is the right word," she answered, "but the truth is math and I don't always get along." She pointed a finger at him. "I bet you're a math whiz."

"Not exactly," he said, "but I do use dimensions, quantities, area and other math-based principles in my work, as they relate to spatial thinking and patterns." He took a breath then gave her another lopsided smile. "From mummy's boy to architecture geek. I'm not doing a bang-up job of impressing you, am I?"

"I wouldn't say that," she muttered, because Keaton uttering building terms had the same effect on her body as another man whispering love words.

"Are you far along in your coursework?"

A familiar twinge of regret zipped across her stomach. "I'm in my second year," she told him. "I took some time off after high school to…travel."

"Visit any interesting places?"

She didn't think the backstage area of every seedy concert venue between Austin and Los Angeles was what he had in mind, so she only shook her head. "Nothing worth mentioning." She took another drink then idly flipped through her study guide. "I'm sorry to say my study break should probably be over now. I really do need to be ready for tomorrow morning."

Was that a look of disappointment that darkened his eyes for a brief moment?

"Thank you again for coming to my rescue tonight."

"No problem. I'm sure your project is going to be great," she answered.

"Would you like an early view of the plans sometime?"

She swallowed. This was her chance. *Say something witty. Something flirty and cute.* "Sure," she answered on a squeak. Okay, that was pathetic.

Keaton didn't seem to notice. "Good luck with your test tomorrow."

She blew out a breath and tucked a stray curl behind one ear. "I'm going to need it."

He slid to the edge of the booth like he was going to ease himself out then stopped. "I could help you study," he offered suddenly. "Quiz you on concepts and such?"

Francesca felt her mouth drop open. "Really? Because I'm sure you have someplace better to be." Obviously he was being kind, but she didn't want him to feel obliged to sit with her. Despite being her best friend, Ciara had made it clear on several occasions how boring Francesca was when she studied.

"I have no plans and there's still…" He glanced at his watch then back at her. "Over an hour until the diner closes." He moved back to the center of the bench seat. "It'll be fun."

"You must have a strange definition of fun in England." She handed him a stack of notecards. "But I can use all the help I can get. Thank you."

He asked the first question and Francesca couldn't hide her smile. Maybe if principles of accounting were spoken in a British accent, she'd enjoy the class more. She made a mental note to buy handsome men slices of pie more often. Already this was the best study session she'd ever had.

Chapter Three

Keaton walked toward the restaurant in downtown Austin where he'd agreed to meet Ben for lunch the next afternoon. The sidewalk was filled with men and women from all different walks of life. There were corporate types in expensive suits hurrying to and from meetings and power lunches that reminded him of being on the streets in London. Although Austin didn't have the same Wild West atmosphere as Houston or Dallas, he still saw plenty of cowboy boots and Wrangler jeans mixed in with the trendy and somewhat casual style favored by most people in the city. It still felt a world away from the quirky neighborhood that housed his latest project and the casual restaurant that was quickly becoming his home away from home.

He'd thought about inviting Ben to Lola May's, but for some reason Keaton wanted to keep the little gem of a diner to himself. It probably had something to do with retaining a bit of his anonymity, or at least keeping the focus on his work or even his accent, and not the craziness that came with being a Fortune.

Growing up in London, Keaton understood that people went a bit wacky for the royals and the Fortunes were their own version of an American royal family. They were particularly well known in Texas. Last year cosmetics mogul Kate Fortune had appointed Keaton's half brother, Graham Fortune Robinson, as CEO of Fortune Cosmetics. That bit of news, coupled with the earlier revelation that Gerald Robinson was really Jerome Fortune, meant a brighter spotlight continued to shine on the branch of the Fortune family from Austin.

It was still an adjustment to be recognized as a Fortune when Keaton had been raised so differently from his half siblings. He liked that the staff and other customers at Lola May's had quickly accepted him as a regular. Since it was just him and his mother growing up, Keaton appreciated any time he could be a part of a bigger community, even the casual kind at Lola May's.

It was a far cry from the night clubs and swanky house parties he was used to back in London and it seemed to fuel his creative side as well as his spirit. He'd stayed up late last night redesigning the residential section that would become the second phase of the Austin Commons project based on feedback he'd received from the development company's CEO. In addition to the brownstones and smaller apartments, he'd added an inner courtyard that could function as a community gathering space.

Many of the changes centered around an open-air design with shade pavilions to take advantage of the mild temperatures in Austin. Granted, he had yet to live through a Texas summer, but he was definitely enjoying the fact that he could be out in just a shirt in January.

He'd spoken to his mother just yesterday, and she'd told him it had rained in London every day since the new year began. Keaton lifted his face to the bright Texas sun and was grateful for the warmth on his skin.

Almost as grateful as he was to the obnoxious local at the diner last night who'd given him an earful of grief. Listening to that blighter was a small price to pay for finally getting an opportunity to talk to Francesca Harriman.

At first she'd been as skittish as one of the colts on Graham's ranch outside of town. The pink that had tinged her cheeks when she'd mentioned his accent was adorable. It was a strange thing, the way American women got so flustered when he spoke. But he had to admit he'd placed an extra emphasis on rounding his vowels and making his voice a bit more clipped when speaking to Francesca just to elicit a reaction from her.

It seemed only fair given the way she made him feel as nervous as a schoolboy with his first crush. He would have been content to sit and stare at her all night long. From a distance it was difficult to notice anything except her riot of blond curls and that luscious figure. Up close he realized her features were quite delicate, from her caramel-colored eyes with flecks of gold dancing through them to her high cheekbones and rosebud mouth.

More surprising was how much he'd enjoyed simply talking to Francesca once they'd each acclimated to the other. He could tell she didn't even realize how appealing she was with her humor and gentle teasing. He was used to women who played games by volleying veiled sexual innuendoes and flirting outrageously. Francesca was wholly real, and helping her study for her test had been the most fun he'd had in ages.

If only he'd had a study partner like Francesca when he'd been at university. Scratch that. He would have spent far too much time watching her nibble on her bottom lip, something she did when concentrating and one more thing about her that drove him absolutely wild.

"Who is she?"

Keaton stopped as his half brother Ben Fortune Robinson stepped in front of him on the sidewalk. He was surprised to realize he'd made it to the restaurant, as he'd been oblivious to any thoughts except those of Francesca.

"I don't know what you're talking about," he lied. "I've got work on the brain."

Although they had different mothers, Keaton looked enough like the Robinson twins, Wes and Ben, to make it clear to any stranger that he was related. Ben had come to London last year after his sister Rachel had revealed that Gerald Robinson was truly Jerome Fortune and the eight legitimate Robinson children might have other half siblings they didn't know from their father's various short-lived affairs over the years. Keaton had never known his father but the photo that Ben had of Gerald showed the same man from the photo Keaton's mother kept hidden in her dresser drawer. The man who had broken her heart.

It had been a shock for Keaton to discover he was part of such a large and famous family, but he was determined to track down the rest of the children Gerald had left in his wake.

Ben was now happily married to Ella, who he'd hired to help him track down Keaton and other possible siblings. The happy couple was expecting their first baby in the next few weeks, which meant that in the course of one short year, Keaton had gone from an only child to a brother and soon-to-be uncle.

He held the door of the cafe open for Ben, who leveled a knowing look at him. "Give me a break," Ben said before greeting the hostess by name. As the young woman led them to a table in the back, Ben continued to goad him. "If designing a building puts that cow-eyed look on your face, you definitely need to get out more."

"I don't know what kind of cows you have in Texas," Keaton shot back, "but I'm not one of them."

Obviously listening to their conversation, the hostess gave him a strange, assessing smile as they sat and she handed them menus.

"I guess you're simply infatuated with our fair city," Ben answered. "We'll leave it at that."

"Good idea," Keaton agreed. He wasn't ready to share Francesca with anyone. They'd only had one conversation, but he wanted more. The trick was going to be how to convince her. "How is Ella?"

"In her words she's 'ready to pop,'"

A waitress approached the table and recited the lunch specials in a bored, monotone voice. Keaton couldn't help compare this place with Lola May's, where the waitstaff and customers joked and laughed and generally treated each other as an extended family. Lola May set the tone for the casual, sociable environment so that eating there felt like pulling up a seat at a friend's table. It was silly, but the restaurant had eased his transition to a new country and unfamiliar city, making him feel like he had a place he belonged.

They ordered and Ben continued, "We have everything set up for the baby's arrival, but I still don't feel ready." He shrugged. "I never thought being a father was in the cards for me, you know?"

Keaton knew all too well. "You'll do great."

"Because I had such a bang-up role model in my dad?" He cleared his throat, then added, "I mean *our* dad."

"Gerald wasn't a father to me," Keaton said quietly. "He isn't anything to me."

The waitress returned with two glasses of iced tea, and he took a long drink to cool the angry heat that pooled low in his stomach at the thought of the man who'd abandoned him and his mother. "But, yes, that's part of the reason why I have no doubt you'll take to fatherhood like a duck to water. It's important for you not to repeat the same mistakes Gerald made."

"I used to believe he'd made mistakes, but now I wonder if he was simply willfully ignorant for so many years." Ben tapped one finger against the table. "Or the type of man who just didn't care."

Keaton inclined his head. "He's still your dad, and I don't want my personal feelings about him to color your opinion."

"Trust me," Ben said quietly, "I've had plenty of reasons to develop my own feelings about him. Each new revelation is a challenge, but Ella has helped me make peace with a lot of it."

"You're lucky to have found her."

"Damn straight. I almost have to be grateful for all the turmoil Dad's new identity caused because it led me to Ella. If I hadn't crashed Kate Fortune's birthday party last year, I never would have met her. It's hard to imagine my life without her. Ella is the best thing that ever happened to me."

"There's another reason you'll be a good father— you love your baby's mother."

"With my whole heart."

Keaton sucked in a sharp breath at Ben's words. What would it feel like to give his whole heart to another person? To him, it felt like a recipe for disaster. He'd seen what that kind of love had done to his mother. She'd never gotten over having her heart broken by Gerald Robinson, and it had colored every part of her life. Keaton wouldn't allow himself to be vulnerable to another person, nor did he want the responsibility of someone loving him that way.

An image of Francesca popped into his mind, but he immediately discounted it. Yes, there was something about the woman that made him want to know her better, but it was infatuation—nothing more.

"Do you have any new leads on other Fortune offspring?" he asked, wanting to change the subject away from love. If Ben was head over heels, there was no sense in Keaton trying to convince his half brother that those feelings were just an illusion. Keaton still worried that he wasn't as distant in personality from Gerald Robinson as he wanted to believe. He simply wasn't built for long-term commitment.

"I'm working on tracking down a woman living right here in Austin. It's a pretty solid lead."

"My contact in France," Keaton said, "is gathering

information about your former au pair. Nothing substantial yet, but he's close. I've also been working to track down another lead in Oklahoma."

Ben gave a small nod. "It's slow going, but that's how we want it. All of these people who my father left behind have lives and families, just like you did. We need to be sure that we approach them the right way."

"It's also important that we're sure they are Gerald's children. There are many reasons someone would want to be part of both the Robinson and the Fortune families." Even before their connection to the Fortunes was revealed, the Robinson family had fame and wealth of their own account. Robinson Computers, the technology company Jerome Fortune founded after he changed his identity to Gerald Robinson, was worth millions and growing every year. Keaton refused to allow his new siblings to fall prey to impostors looking to make a quick buck off a feigned familial connection. But for the ones out there like him...

His thoughts were interrupted as the waitress brought their food. Keaton bit into his hamburger with little appetite. He hated to think other men and women had grown up feeling the lack of a father the same way he had. At the same time, if he could connect with them now, maybe he could ease some of that inherent loneliness.

He wanted to believe he was doing it to help others, but it was as much for himself. His eight half siblings had grown up with Gerald Robinson as their father. Gerald was far from perfect, and had too many secrets, including his true identity, but Kieran, Graham, Ben, Wes, Rachel, Zoe, Olivia and Sophie had always known who they were and where they came from.

Keaton longed to talk to someone who'd shared his experience of longing to know where he belonged.

He and Ben discussed more specifics about how to track down the other half siblings as they ate, then Keaton headed across town to the office of Ariana Lamonte, a reporter at *Weird Life Magazine*, who had emailed him with an interview request regarding a story she was doing on the Fortune family.

Ben had warned Keaton to check her out before he agreed to anything. The Fortunes were big news in Texas, which was why Keaton didn't speak to many people about his relationship with the family. He had a well-honed protective streak, thanks to years of taking care of his mum. In fact, it still shocked him that he'd shared so much of his history last night with Francesca. Yet there was something about her that made him confident he could trust her.

Whether he could trust the reporter remained to be seen. He walked the half dozen blocks to the magazine's trendy office. Clouds had rolled in while he was having lunch and a brisk breeze was beginning to kick up.

Ariana Lamonte met him in the lobby and led him to a small conference room. He wasn't sure what he expected from the reporter, but the friendly woman with long brown hair, wearing a brightly patterned dress and chunky jewelry wasn't it. He'd been skeptical as to the blogger's motivations for wanting to interview him, but his gut told him he could trust this woman. As he lowered himself into the chair across from her, she opened the file folder and began to spread out photos on the table between them.

"Thank you for agreeing to meet with me," she said, her smile genuine.

"You realize I haven't yet agreed to anything more?" he asked. He relied on his instincts about people but his own feelings about being a Fortune made him wary of discussing the family with anyone who wasn't in his close circle of confidants. Interesting that Francesca had breached his walls in only one conversation. No one had done that in a long time, and he wasn't sure what it meant about his connection to the plucky waitress.

Ariana didn't seem put off by his question. "I want to reassure you I intend to approach this series of blogs with the utmost respect to your family. The Fortunes are important in Texas, and the family's history appeals to many readers even beyond Austin. I'm curious what it's like to discover that you are part of such a venerable legacy."

He schooled his features as he thought of Gerald's legacy. Yes, Ben and his siblings, the legitimate heirs to the Robinson name, were a big part of that. Each of them had dealt with their own issues since they'd learned that their father was really Jerome Fortune. There was also Charlotte Robinson to consider. Keaton couldn't help but wonder how Gerald's wife of more than thirty years was adjusting to this turn in her family's dynamic. From the little he'd heard from his siblings about their mother, Charlotte was handling the changes with stoic poise, but it had to be acutely difficult for her.

"There are those who have had a bigger adjustment than me," he answered. "You seem to have done your research on the family."

Ariana smoothed a hand over the stack of files that sat in front of her. "I have."

"As I'm sure you know, I was raised by a single mother. That means I always knew there was a part of my history that was missing. For some of the Fortune heirs, I believe it's been quite a shock to discover there is more to their family than they'd grown up knowing."

"But it must have been a shock for you to find out that the father you never knew was actually part of such a well-known and powerful family?"

Keaton inclined his head. "Yes," he admitted.

"That's the focus of this series. I want to profile some of the newer members of the Fortune family and share with readers the unique process of becoming a Fortune."

"Becoming a Fortune," Keaton repeated.

"That's the title of the series," Ariana told him. She slid several of the photos toward him, and he recognized the people in them as other recently minted Fortunes. There were several images of the children of Josephine Fortune Chesterfield. Unlike Gerald, Lady Josephine and her sister, Jeanne Marie Fortune Jones, hadn't kept their status as Fortunes a secret. The women had both been put up for adoption as babies, two of a trio of triplets that also included family scion James Marshall Fortune.

It was only a few years ago that Jeanne Marie and Josephine's connection to the Fortunes was revealed and they and their children had made the transition to being part of the famous family. Keaton already knew of the Fortune Chesterfields, as their ties to the royal family made them celebrities in Britain. From what he'd learned of the Fortune Jones branch of the Fortune family, based in the small Texas town of Horse-back Hollow, they'd been regular people who had a bigger adjustment to being part of the limelight that came from being a Fortune.

"Which of the Fortunes have you spoken to already?"

Ariana's dark gaze didn't waver. "You're the first."

"Why me?"

She held up a hand to tick off the reasons on her fingers. "You're now a local, which will be interesting to my readers, and the Austin Commons project is already news. The fact that you discovered your relationship with Gerald Robinson—or Jerome Fortune to be more precise—as an adult is intriguing. The Fortunes are quite well known in the States, particularly in Texas. The Fortune Chesterfields are famous in their own right, but you're different." She flashed a wry grin and added, "Unique."

"Not as unique as you might think," he muttered then regretted speaking the words out loud when Ariana leaned over the table.

"What does that mean?"

He thought about ignoring the question and refusing to be a part of the interview and subsequent profile. Other than recognition for his work, Keaton had never craved fame. But he remained deeply committed to discovering the others out there who'd been discarded by Gerald, and he felt certain there were more. Maybe if he spoke with Ariana, he could shake up the family tree a bit and see what else might fall from the branches.

He had to balance his need to locate other Fortune children with his desire to respect his half siblings and what the knowledge of their father's philandering would do to them. That meant he had to tread carefully with Ariana.

"It means there's more to the story of Jerome Fortune than anyone outside the family knows."

The reporter's eyes widened and she reached into the purse that sat on the chair next to her and pulled out a hand-held recorder. "What can you tell me?"

"Nothing while we're on the record," he said, shaking his head.

She sucked in a breath, clearly frustrated with his answer. "I have a responsibility to my readers."

"I have a responsibility to my brothers and sisters," he told her. His lungs expanded as he said the words. They were a truth he felt from the bottom of his heart. He might be new to the Fortune family, but Ben, Wes, Graham, Olivia, Rachel, Kieran, Zoe and Sophie meant something to him. They meant he wasn't alone in the world any longer. "I'll talk to you about my theories on Gerald Robinson and the implied consequences of how he's chosen to live his life, but that can't be part of the story you publish."

Ariana studied him for several moments then placed the recorder back in her purse. "Will you agree to a featured profile on you in the magazine and on the blog?"

"I'll think about it."

"What about your theories on your father?"

"He's not—" The urge to deny his connection to Gerald came fast and hot, but he swallowed it back, letting the bitterness burn a path down his throat. "For now, let's just say that I don't think I'm the only skeleton in Gerald's adulterous closet."

"That's quite the bombshell," she murmured.

"Indeed. I plan to uncover my father's secrets."

"I can help," Ariana offered immediately.

He started to protest, but she held up a hand. "Off the record, Keaton. I won't lie to you, if the 'Becoming a Fortune' series takes off, it will be a great stepping stone for me. I'm good at research and tracking down leads. But I'll only take it as far as makes you and your half siblings comfortable. All I ask in return is that you agree to let me interview you, and not block my way to speaking with other Fortunes."

"That's fair," he agreed then glanced at his watch. "I have a meeting at my office this afternoon. Call me and we'll set up a time to talk about my Fortune journey."

She stood at the same time he did and they shook hands. "I look forward to it," she told him.

He expected to feel tense about what he'd agreed to, but as he returned to the Austin Commons project site, a sense of peace descended over him. He could try to convince himself and everyone around him that Gerald meant nothing to him, but the lack of a father had shaped almost every decision Keaton had made in his life. This was his chance to define what "becoming a Fortune" meant to him, and if Ariana Lamonte could help track down other half siblings then all the better.

Chapter Four

When the bell above the door to Lola May's chimed at just past six that evening, Francesca didn't need to turn around to know that Keaton had just walked in. The fact that her heart began to race and a tiny shiver made goose bumps pop up all over her body left no question.

She smiled at the couple at the table in front of her as she set down their plates of food. The man made a silly joke about buttering biscuits and Francesca tried to think of a clever response. She liked bantering with customers, but right now every one of her brain cells had taken the fast train south to parts of her body she'd assumed were stuck in permanent hibernation.

Keaton Whitfield might be the reason for global warming, at least in Francesca's world.

Glancing out of the corner of her eye, she saw him

slide into a booth in her section. It shouldn't be so difficult to think about speaking to him. They'd had an entire conversation last night where she hadn't stuttered or drooled or made an obvious idiot of herself. He'd been polite and charming, neither of which surprised her given how she'd seen him interact with Lola May and the other waitresses during his daily visits to the diner.

But actually *enjoying* his company had been a bit of a revelation. She couldn't remember ever simply having fun with Lou. Every moment they'd been together had been about her adoring him. His life. His band. His schedule. His needs.

She was still embarrassed to admit how easy it had been to ignore her own needs in trying to take care of him. She knew it stemmed from the fact that she'd grown up without a father. When she'd asked her mother why her dad had left, the answer was always the same—"I couldn't give him what he needed."

Francesca had been determined to give Lou everything he needed so she'd never lose him. The problem was she'd lost herself in the process.

Ciara had the section next to Francesca's on this shift, so it would be easy to beg her friend to take care of Keaton. She stole another glance and found him watching her. A slow, sexy half smile curved one side of his mouth. She was positive he knew that she'd been planning to ditch him. Seriously, it was like the man was some sort of British mind reader.

How difficult could it be to serve him a meal? It was her job, after all, and they'd already had a conversation. No biggie, right?

"Hi," she said as she approached the booth and

wondered if that one word sounded as lame to him as it did to her.

"Hello, Francesca," he said in that gorgeous accent. He might as well have said "I'd like to ravish you" because all her circuits went slightly haywire. "You look lovely tonight."

She glanced down at her black Lola May's T-shirt and the denim skirt she'd paired with pink cowboy boots. She had a small splattering of ketchup just above the letter *M* that made her feel the exact opposite of lovely.

"How was your test?" he asked.

She met his gaze and promptly forgot how to speak. It was as if the English language didn't exist to her anymore. All she could do was stare and—oh, dear— was that yearning she felt? She could almost feel her body *yearning* for the man. Not a good sign. Francesca had vowed to become strong and independent after her break up with Lou, but now her fledgling feelings for Keaton made her feel flustered and weak in the knees. She couldn't risk being weak ever again.

She groaned softly then realized Keaton was still watching her. Wait, what had he asked her just now?

He ran a hand over his jaw and the slight rasping of stubble against skin did nothing to help her focus. How would his face feel under her fingertips? What if she kissed the edge of his jaw?

"You did have a test today?" he prompted.

She blinked. Swallowed. Made a fist and dug her fingernails into the fleshy part of her palm, hoping that the bite of pain might help her focus.

"Test," she repeated like a googly-eyed tween when faced with her biggest fangirl crush.

"Accounting, I believe?"

"Yes, accounting." She licked her dry lips and his gaze zeroed in on her mouth. Not helping her focus. "I think it went well. I don't have my grade yet but I hope it went well. I hope…"

That you'll take off your shirt right now.

Nope. She certainly wasn't going to add that.

"I hope you're hungry," she said instead.

Keaton's smile widened and Francesca felt a blush rise to her cheeks. "For dinner," she added and grabbed the small pad of paper from the pocket in her apron. "Are you ready to order?"

"What's the special?"

Me was the first answer that popped into Francesca's mind and she wanted to wring her own neck. She knew better than to let her attraction to a man overwhelm her. She'd been down that road before, the one where she felt grateful for any crumbs of attention. On the surface, Keaton had nothing in common with Lou the Louse, but they were both men who were way out of her league. Why pretend it was any different?

"Chicken pot pie. It's a recipe from Lola May's grandmother. We make the crust from scratch. It's amazing."

"I'm game for some amazing," he told her. "Pot pie it is."

"Anything to drink?"

"Water is fine. Is there a chance you could take a break and keep me company while I eat?"

She glanced around at the crowded diner. "It's only Ciara and me on shift tonight so…" She wanted to take a break with his man. She wanted a lot more, too. "I'll try."

"Smashing," he murmured.

She giggled at the obviously British term then clasped a hand over her mouth. Francesca had been around the block enough to know better than to be turned into a giggling school girl because a handsome man with a dashing accent showed her a bit of attention.

Another customer waved her down and she hurried away, her heart still racing. Why was it so difficult to act normal with Keaton?

She gave his order for the kitchen then delivered a glass of water to his table. He was frowning at something on his phone as she approached. When he glanced up at her, there was a momentary look of such pain in his eyes that she hurt for him. It took all her willpower not to slip in next to him in the booth and give him a hug, nerves be damned. He looked like he needed a hug as much as he needed his next breath.

He closed his eyes for a second and when he opened them, the look was gone. She started to ask about it, but the toddler in the booth behind him knocked over her juice, so Francesca quickly grabbed a pile of napkins to help clean up the mess.

A few minutes later, Keaton's pot pie was ready. She picked up the plate from the pass through between the kitchen and the front of the restaurant. There was no way she was going to get a break before closing, so she thought about asking Keaton if he could stick around until her shift was over. She wanted to spend time with him, but the very thought of it made her heart hammer and her palms sweat.

Sweaty palms and carrying a porcelain plate were not a good combination apparently. When Keaton looked up and flashed another one of those sexy half smiles, the plate started to slip out of Francesca's hand. She leaned over the booth, trying to will the plate to land on the table, which it did. But it had so much momentum that it skidded to the edge and tipped off, dumping the entire hot, steaming mass of pot pie into Keaton's lap.

He made a choked sound and Francesca gasped. She'd been waiting tables since she was sixteen and had never dumped food into a customer's lap.

The next few minutes were a blur. The only thing she was sure of was that she'd never been more humiliated. She bent toward him, reaching for his lap at the same time Keaton straightened from the booth. The top of his head clipped her chin, and she gave a tiny yelp as she bit down on her tongue.

"I'm sorry, luv," he said immediately, but she was intent on cleaning up the mess she made.

So intent that she grabbed the hunk of food from his lap before the realization hit her that she was basically pawing at his crotch.

She let out a little screech and her hand jerked, sending chunks of chicken and bits of carrot and corn onto his shirt front.

"I'm so sorry," she muttered, but before he could respond, Lola May was at her side with a wet rag.

"Customers want to eat the food, Frannie, not wear it."

"I didn't mean—"

"Go get yourself cleaned up," Lola May snapped and Francesca glanced down at the dripping mess of pot pie she held in her hand.

"I'm sorry," she said again without meeting Keaton's

crystal-blue gaze. How could she ever look at him again after this fiasco?

She ran to the back of the restaurant, washing her hands under the faucet of the kitchen's utility sink. Pieces of crust and dollops of gravy clung to her T-shirt, making the ketchup spot she'd worried over earlier seem invisible.

"You smell like dinner," the head cook, Richard, told her with a laugh.

"It's not funny," she answered. "I made a huge mess of a customer."

"From what I've heard from the other waitresses," the older man said, "that British bloke has a thing for you. Maybe he figured dumping food in his lap was your way of flirting. Tell him it's an American custom."

Francesca groaned. "I'm not telling him anything. I doubt he'll ever want to speak with me again."

The thought made tears prick the backs of her eyes, and she bit down on her lip. Lola May kept a shelf of diner T-shirts for the tourists who wanted to purchase them, so Francesca went to the bathroom and changed.

She stepped out into the hallway just as Ciara turned the corner. "You have to take my tables," she whispered to her friend. "I can't go back out there. It's too embarrassing."

"I have a full section of my own, so you're stuck back on the floor, sweetie. It may even improve your tips. Customers will be scared that if they aren't nice, you'll dump food on them, too." Ciara chuckled. "That was definitely impressive aim."

"You know that was an accident. Why does everyone think it's funny?" Francesca covered her face with her hands. "I bet he doesn't think it's funny, and I can guarantee Lola May isn't amused."

"True about Lola May," Ciara admitted. "Keaton was a good sport about the whole thing, though, and we packed up a new pot pie in a to-go box for him so he'll be fine."

Francesca peeked through her fingers. "He's gone?"

Ciara nodded. "He smelled like 'winner winner chicken pot pie dinner.' Did you expect him to stay for a second helping?"

"Of course not. How could I have been so clumsy?" She pointed at Ciara. "This fiasco is why I should have asked you to take his table. I'm a bumbling idiot when it comes to that man."

"Maybe he finds it adorable, like you're some kind of quirky sitcom star."

"Or maybe he thinks I'm an idiot girl who can't even put together a coherent sentence when talking to a handsome man." She leaned her head back against the tiled wall. "I feel like such a fool," she muttered. "As usual."

"It was pot pie, Francesca. You didn't light his pants on fire." Ciara stepped forward. "Keaton Whitfield likes you. Don't overthink it. Don't let Lou the Louse get in your head."

"What does that mean?"

"Your ex-boyfriend did a number on you. He made you believe you were lucky to be with him. Lou's world revolved around Lou, and yours had to, as well. That's no way to have a relationship."

"But I was—"

"Way more than the Louse deserved," Ciara interrupted. She wrapped Francesca in a tight hug. "Keaton sees something in you, and the man's not stupid. Maybe it's time you believe you're enough just the way you are, clumsy episodes with pot pie and all."

Francesca let out a strangled laugh. "That might have been the single most embarrassing moment of my life."

"At least you made an impression. He'll never forget you. Who knows, maybe you two will serve chicken pot pie at your wedding reception someday."

"Before I start with wedding plans, I should probably work on figuring out how to speak to him without losing my mind."

"Actually," Ciara answered, taking a step back, "you might want to start with a shower. No offense, girlfriend, but you stink."

"Put those plans for a shower on the back burner," Lola May shouted from the end of the hallway. "Our customers have been kept waiting long enough. Come on, you two. We have a full house and this food won't serve itself."

Francesca followed Ciara back toward the front of the restaurant, retying her ponytail as she walked.

"I'm sorry," she whispered to Lola May as she passed. "I'll pay for the food and his dry cleaning."

"Let's just get through the rest of your shift with no more accidents." The diner owner patted Francesca's arm.

"You're not mad?"

Lola May rolled her eyes. "I'm an old woman who only recently found the courage to leave a crappy marriage behind. I'm living vicariously through your little...whatever...with Keaton. Dumping a plate of food in a potential suitor's lap isn't exactly the way

I would have gone, but I'm curious to see where this episode takes you."

Francesca sucked in a breath. "It was an accident."

"I know," Lola May said and gave her a gentle push forward. "But it's also a potential opportunity. Let's see what you do with it."

Keaton rubbed his fingers against his temples as he looked up from his computer the following afternoon. He was alone in the on-site office at the Austin Commons project, having just finished a marathon meeting with the general contractor and the structural engineer.

In the best of all possible worlds, every part of designing a building would go smoothly, from the concept to the plans to actually breaking ground. In reality his business, much like his current personal life, was rarely that straightforward.

The contractor had asked one of the other architects on the project to tweak the roof design of the main retail space, which the junior-level associate had done without clearing with Keaton. Now the structural engineer had discovered an issue with the truss design and the load-bearing walls. It was up to Keaton to figure out a way to fix the problem without slowing the project or pulling additional funds from the budget.

A knock on the modular trailer's metal door had him gritting his teeth. Keaton wasn't in the mood for any more issues today, and every time someone walked through that door it felt like more work got piled on his shoulders.

"Come in," he called reluctantly, because it wasn't as if he could hide in here forever.

His heart gave a tiny leap when Francesca entered

the trailer, her wild mane of blond curls tumbling over her shoulders. She wore it up at the diner, and this was the first time he'd seen the curls in all their glory.

He was mesmerized.

She offered a tentative smile. "I hope I'm not interrupting something important."

He scrambled up from the desk chair, the training his mother had given him on standing when a woman entered the room automatically guiding his movements. "Not at all." Striding forward, he narrowly missed tripping over the waste bin next to the desk.

Francesca took a quick step back as he hurtled toward her, holding aloft the cardboard box tied with a piece of twine she held in her hands.

"It's bad enough I dumped dinner on you," she said with a nervous laugh. "I don't want to smash my apology pie against your chest."

He righted himself, feeling color creep along the collar of his oxford-cloth shirt. What was it about this woman that made him as jumpy as a wet-behind-the-ears lad? Given the fact that he'd gone home last night smelling like Sunday dinner, he could at least take comfort that he wasn't the only one affected.

"There's no need to apologize," he said as she lowered the box. "Although I won't say no to a slice of Lola May's pie."

He saw her fingers tighten slightly on the box, and she gave him another shy smile. "This is actually my pie," she told him. "It's the chocolate pecan recipe my mom makes for Thanksgiving." Her pert nose wrinkled. "She considers it a once-a-year treat. Little does she know I make it every time I need a pick-me-up. I call it Pick-Me-Up Pecan Pie."

"How did you know I needed a lift today?"

"I knew I needed to apologize," she said as an answer. "Pie works for that purpose, too." She shoved the box toward him. "I'm truly sorry about last night. I've been waitressing a lot of years and nothing like that has ever happened. I hope you'll allow me to pay for your clothes to be dry cleaned or replaced."

"No need," he told her. "I actually owe you a thank you. My neighbor has a dog that's been skittish with me since I moved in. They were coming back from a walk last night when I got home, and now the pup and I are best mates." He shrugged. "My scent was irresistible."

She laughed softly, and the sound was just as irresistible. "I'm glad my disaster had a silver lining for you."

"The dog wasn't the silver lining." He tapped one finger on the top of the box. "You and pie are the silver lining. I hope you have time to have a piece with me?" He leaned in. "You know it's bad luck to eat pie alone."

She made a sound that was half laugh and half sigh. "That might explain some of the luck I've had in life. I hate to admit the amount of pie I've eaten on my own."

His heart twisted as a pain she couldn't quite hide flared in those caramel eyes. His well-honed protective streak kicked in, but it was also more than that. He wanted to take up the sword and go to battle against whatever dragons had hurt this lovely, vibrant woman.

It was an idiotic notion, both because Francesca had never given him any indication that she needed assistance slaying dragons and because he didn't have the genetic makeup of a hero. Not with Gerald Robinson as his father.

But he couldn't quite make himself walk away from the chance to give her what whatever he could that might once again put a smile on her beautiful face.

"Then it's time for a dose of good luck." He stepped back and pulled out a chair at the small, scuffed conference table in the center of the office. "I can't think of a better way to begin than with a slice of Pick-Me-Up Pecan Pie. Join me?"

Her gaze darted to the door before settling on him. "Yes, thank you," she murmured and dropped into the seat.

Her scent drifted up to him—vanilla and spice, perfect for the type of woman who would bake a pie from scratch. He'd never considered baking to be a particularly sexy activity, but the thought of Francesca wearing an apron in the kitchen as she mixed ingredients for his pie made sparks dance across his skin.

The mental image changed to Francesca wearing nothing but an apron and—

"I have plates," he shouted and she jerked back in the chair.

"That's helpful," she answered quietly, giving him a curious look. "Do you have forks, too?"

"Yes, forks." He turned toward the small bank of cabinets installed in one corner of the trailer. "And napkins," he called over his shoulder. Damn, he sounded like a complete prat.

He took a breath, did some calculating of dimensions and slope in his head until his body was under control again. Then he pulled out two paper plates, plastic forks, napkins and a knife from the drawer.

Francesca had taken off her pale blue cardigan sweater by the time he returned to the table. Under it she wore a sleeveless floral-patterned dress with a demure neckline.

It was warm in the trailer, and the glimpse of the smooth skin of her shoulders caused Keaton to feel downright hot.

Get a grip, he told himself.

She was already jittery around him. The desire he had to kiss her senseless every time he looked at her wasn't going to help her nerves.

He focused on the task at hand, untying the knot on the top of the box, lifting the lid to reveal a pie that could only be described as work of art—at least to a pie aficionado like Keaton.

"You made this?"

She nodded. "It's a traditional pecan pie but the bittersweet chocolate adds a bit of depth and I also add a splash of bourbon. Don't tell my mom, but I think the flavor of my pie is one step above hers." She pressed her fingers to her cheeks, cringing slightly. "I mean, not that I assume you're going to meet my mom or anything."

"If it tastes anything like it looks," he said, ignoring her adorable bout with nerves as he sliced the pie, "I'll bet it's once step up from heaven."

"Have you always been addicted to pie?" she asked with a laugh.

"*Addicted* is such an ugly word," he answered. "I prefer being called a connoisseur." She grinned and all the problems that had seemed so insurmountable a few minutes ago slipped away like sand through an hourglass. "My mother's specialty is bread pudding. She makes the occasional apple tart but not many sweet pies."

She held up one of the plates and he slid a generous slice onto it. "I'll have one half that size," she told him, "or else I'm going to end up on the treadmill for an extra thirty minutes tonight."

"I can't imagine that," he said but cut a smaller piece for the second plate.

"I don't eat much pie these days," she admitted. "You know what they say—a moment on the lips means—" She clapped a hand over her mouth. The light he'd come to rely on in her eyes dimmed the tiniest bit. "Never mind."

"I don't know what they say." He took the seat next to her. "Tell me."

She shook her head. "Even I should know better than to talk about weight with a man."

"Please," he added, both because he was genuinely curious and also because he didn't like any saying that took away some of the brightness he associated with Francesca.

"A moment on the lips," she repeated quietly, "means a lifetime on the hips."

He paused with the fork halfway to his mouth. "I certainly hope you are not disparaging your hips in any manner. I don't want to overstep the bounds of what is appropriate conversation, but your body is perfect, Francesca."

Two splotches of captivating pink color bloomed on her cheeks. "Thank you," she whispered. "I had two nicknames when I was growing up—Frizzy Frannie and Fat Frannie. I refuse to revisit either of those."

He set down his fork and reached out to touch her

hair. He'd wanted to trail his fingers through it since the moment she'd walked in, and the thick strands were just as soft as he'd imagined. "You have the kind of hair that would make angels jealous."

She blushed even deeper but gave him a smile so brilliant he felt the glow of it to his toes. "Angel hair and heavenly pie. Are all British men so charming?"

"Not all," he told her. "I'm one in a million."

She threw back her head and laughed out loud at that. "Eat your pie." She pointed to his plate. "Pie heaven is setting the bar pretty high. I'm curious to see how I did."

He reluctantly dropped his fingers from her hair and took a bite. The sugary filling practically melted in his mouth and he bit down on the roasted pecans, which had a rich, smoky flavor. The crust was flaky and the bourbon added just the right bit of tang. All in all it was...

"Heavenly," he murmured.

"You don't have to say that," she said and took a forkful of her own slice.

"I know, but it's true. Pick-Me-Up Pecan Pie is perfect."

She smiled. "It's a lot of *p*'s, but I like the sound of it."

"You're a pie-naming genius," Keaton said softly and was rewarded with more blushing from Francesca. She had the body of a nineteen fifties pinup girl and the full mouth of a sexy screen siren, but the brief glimpses of her innocence were what really drove him wild. Francesca Harriman was a puzzle Keaton needed to solve. "Does Lola May know you bake like this?"

Francesca shrugged. "She makes all the pies for the restaurant. I'm just a waitress."

"How long have you worked there?"

"Off and on since I was sixteen. Lola May runs the show, and she takes great pride in her pies. She's a good boss and is willing to be flexible with my shifts based on my course load each semester."

"Do you have other pies in your repertoire or is pecan the pièce de résistance?"

She smiled. "My mom taught me to bake when I was little. Rolling out the perfect crust was the first lesson. There are a few other types of pies I bake."

"How convenient," he said. "Because there are plenty of other pies I'd like to try. I bet they all have creative names, too."

"Most of them," she admitted.

"Such as…"

"There's a triple berry pie called The Berry Bomb and I make a strawberry rhubarb pie in the summer that's aptly named The Sweettart." She ducked her chin and looked up at him through her lashes. "Kind of silly, but it's fun to name them."

"It's cute, just like you." He broke off a piece of crust and popped it into his mouth. "I'm not much of a baker, but I make a pretty fantastic spaghetti Bolognese. One of these nights, I'll cook dinner for you and you can impress me with another selection of pie."

Francesca's eyes widened at the same time her mouth dropped open. She stared at him for a moment then placed her fork on the table, pulled her sweater around her shoulders and practically jumped out of the chair.

Damn. He'd gone too far, too fast.

"I—I should let you get back to work," she stammered. He wanted to argue but was afraid of unnerving her more than he already had.

Once some of her initial tension had disappeared, she'd been funny and flirtatious. He wanted more of that. He wanted to know the name of anyone who had dared to call her fat, when her body was perfect in every way. He'd wanted to hear about how she'd been raised and if being the child of a single mother had made her into the person she was today, as it had him.

"Would you like a tour of the project site?" he blurted, trying to think of something—anything— to keep her with him. Yes, he had plenty of work he was ignoring. But right now all he cared about was convincing Francesca to give him a few more minutes of her time. As she mulled over how to answer, he moved behind the desk and grabbed the 3D model of Austin Commons off a shelf. "We're not too far on the building process, but this will show you the overall vision."

She stepped forward and drew in a small breath. "It's cool," she whispered, "like a real-life dollhouse."

Keaton smiled. If she wanted to compare hours of developing renderings in order to transfer the computer-aided design files to scale to be printed with the firm's highly detailed 3D printer to building a child's dollhouse, he'd let her. "A really precisely scaled dollhouse," he murmured.

"I sound silly," she said, making a face. "I know it's not as simple as a dollhouse."

He pushed the pie box to one side of the table and

set the model in the center. Francesca picked up their two empty plates, forks and napkins and dumped them into the trash bin before returning to his side.

"Can I touch it?" she asked then gave a muffled laugh. "The model, I mean."

He managed to keep a straight face as he answered, "Of course."

"Did you always know you wanted to be an architect?" She placed one finger on the edge of the paper roof and bent so that she was at eye level with his design.

"For as long as I can remember, I liked to build things. My mum worked in a manufacturing plant and she'd bring all different sizes of cardboard boxes home for me. I created elaborate cardboard cities that spanned the length of the living room. Mum was quite patient." He crouched down so he had the same view as Francesca. "I didn't play with dollhouses, but those boxes were an early version of what I'm doing here."

"It's wonderful."

"Yes," he answered but Keaton wasn't talking about the model.

She turned her head, so close that he could see the golden flecks around the edges of her eyes. It would be so easy to lean in and brush his mouth against hers. Her tongue darted out to wet her bottom lip and he had to stifle a groan.

"I'd like to see the rest," she said softly.

Keaton figured he must be the biggest pervert on the planet, because everything that came out of Francesca's mouth sounded like sexual innuendo. He did his best to tamp down the need for her that surged through him like a raging river. If she was spooked by an off-hand comment about dinner, all the other things he wanted to say would terrify her to pieces.

He forced himself to straighten and held out a hand. "Let's find you a hard hat and we'll begin the tour."

Chapter Five

"Y̲ou asked him if you could touch it?" Ciara asked later that afternoon, stifling a laugh.

Francesca groaned. "Everything that came out of my mouth made me sound like I was desperate for sex."

"Did you tell him how big it looked?" Ciara giggled. "Men like to talk about size."

"Stop," Francesca shouted, even though her friend was sitting right beside her on the sofa. Francesca was working the dinner shift at Lola May's so she had stopped home after the tour with Keaton to change clothes and grab some food. "You're making it worse."

"It doesn't actually sound too bad," her roommate answered. "You brought him one of your scrumptious pies and engaged in a little harmless flirting."

"He kind of hinted that he'd like to cook dinner for me."

"Did you say yes?" Ciara asked. "A thousand times yes?" she added, quoting their favorite Jane Austen movie remake.

"Not exactly," Francesca admitted. "I kind of almost bolted for the door."

She let out a yelp when Ciara gave her a hard shove. "That man *likes* you with a capital *L*. I'd even use the other *L* word."

"Ciara, stop."

"Lust, Frankie," Ciara clarified with a wink. "I'm talking about lust. You've got to pull your head out of your—"

"My head is just fine where it is," Francesca argued.

Ciara sniffed and flipped a lock of glossy hair over her shoulder. Francesca had given up comparing her mass of blond curls with Ciara's silky straight mane years ago. They were opposites in looks, but Francesca knew her friend had similar issues with men, so Ciara understood Francesca's reluctance to get involved in a relationship again.

"I'm not talking about heavy-duty commitment," Ciara continued, as if reading Francesca's mind. "I mean a few fun dates and maybe a little swapping of spit for good measure."

Francesca cringed. "That's gross."

"I can guarantee nothing about it would be gross with Keaton."

Francesca thought about the moment in his office earlier today when their faces had been so close she could make out the beginning hint of the day's stubble across his jaw. She'd wanted him to kiss her but had also been terrified that he might and she wouldn't measure up.

"Lou is the only man I've ever...you know." She didn't regret her inexperience but could almost guarantee Keaton normally dated women far more worldly than her.

"Lou the Louse was a boy," Ciara answered. "Or at best a man-child. He could barely blow his nose if you weren't holding the tissue. Keaton is a man. He'll know how to treat a woman. He'd be good for you, Frankie. Having some fun would be good for you."

Ciara liked to throw the word *fun* at Francesca like she was drowning in an ocean of boring and fun was her only lifeline.

"Doesn't it sound like fun to spend four years traveling the country with an indie-rock band?" Francesca asked, picking at a loose thread in the sofa's seam. "My time with Lou was supposed to be a great adventure, but there was precious little fun in it for me."

Ciara pressed her lips together then whispered, "That is not your fault."

"It was my fault that I stayed for so long," Francesca argued. "Now I've got my head on straight and my life together. Finally. I have a plan, Ci. Fun is all well and good, but it's not going to give me a stable future."

"You're too young to be thinking about stability."

Francesca almost laughed at that comment. She'd been thinking about stability since she was a young girl. Her mom had had a difficult time holding down steady work, and as a result, for several years they'd bounced around to several low-rent apartments in shoddy neighborhoods. Francesca had attended five different schools before landing at the high school where she'd met Lou. She'd been blinded by his reputation and appeal for far too long but now she knew the only way to true happiness was depending on herself.

"At least promise you won't shut him down without giving the two of you a chance," Ciara pleaded.

"Fine," Francesca agreed. "It's not like I have a ton of free time, anyway." She glanced at her watch. "I need to get downstairs. Have fun tonight." She gave Ciara a quick hug and stood. "Wear your heaviest jacket. The temperature was dropping fast when I came home."

"What would I do without you to take care of me?" Ciara asked with a laugh. "Miles, Jaycee and I are going to dinner, then hitting that new dance club over on Martin Street. Why don't you join us after you close?"

"I need to study," Francesca answered automatically.

"Not every night." Ciara frowned. "You can take a little time off."

As close as the two women were, this was an ongoing argument, and Francesca knew better than to think she could win it. "Maybe," she said.

Ciara nodded. "One of these days maybe is going to turn into yes."

After Francesca head toward the stairs, she dabbed on a bit of lip-gloss. She didn't usually bother with makeup when she worked—or at all—but the thought that Keaton would be eating at the diner tonight gave her an extra incentive.

It was almost eight before he walked into the restaurant. She was taking the drink order of a party of four, but felt his gaze and glanced over. He went to a corner table in her section and raised a brow, as if asking her permission.

She gave a small nod and returned her attention to the foursome. A few minutes later, she approached Keaton's table and set down a glass of water.

"The special tonight is lasagna," she told him, "so I'll try not to spill tomato sauce all over you." She tested out a grin, feeling her smile widen as Keaton returned it with one of his own. "That stuff stains."

"It would be worth it if I got another pie for my trouble." He reached out and placed one finger on her wrist. "And an afternoon with you."

The butterflies were back in full force at his touch. They swooped and fluttered around her belly and up into her chest, making it difficult to gather a breath.

"Maybe we'll have to arrange that without the mess," she told him. *Maybe* with Keaton meant something different than it had when she'd said the word to Ciara. It meant yes.

He ordered the lasagna and a salad. Francesca managed to bring both to him without incident. She also brought him a slice of Lola May's Dutch apple pie, and he lingered over the dessert until the restaurant was empty except for him.

Just before Lola May was ready to lock the front door, Ciara burst through with her posse of friends. Francesca had hung out with Miles and his girlfriend, Jaycee, several times when they'd come up to the apartment before a night out. They were boisterous and energetic, always on the lookout for the next good time.

They were like a lot of people Francesca knew in Austin. The town was a unique mix of cowboy culture, a hip urban vibe and a bit of the eclectic strangeness that gave the town its famous slogan—"Keep Austin Weird." To Francesca it had always been home, but sometimes she felt like she wasn't quite cool enough to deserve the label of Austinite.

"It's freezing out there," Jaycee said, jumping up and down.

"It feels more like Chicago than Austin," Miles agreed, clasping his hands together and blowing on them.

Ciara walked up to Francesca and wrapped her in a frigid hug. Normally the temps hovered in the mid-fifties during the winter in Austin, so it was a big deal when it dipped to the freezing mark. "We stopped by to see if you want to come out with us."

Francesca shook her head. "I'm going to help Lola May close up and…" She darted a glance at Keaton, who was casually watching the scene with Ciara and her friends.

"*Maybe* you'll get a better offer." Ciara wiggled her brows. "I won't be late," she said and gave Francesca another hug. "Wait up because I definitely want to hear what happens."

"Be safe," Francesca said and realized she sounded more like Ciara's mother than her best friend. She really *had* forgotten how to have fun.

"Lola May," Ciara shouted. "Is it okay if I grab a couple cookies?"

"You betcha, sweetie." Lola May came out from the kitchen, wiping her hands on her apron. "The chocolate chips will keep you warm tonight."

Ciara laughed and took two individually wrapped cookies from the covered cake stand on the diner's counter. "Dancing the night away is what's going to keep me warm."

After blowing Francesca a quick kiss, she followed her friends out into the night. A moment later, Miles poked his head back into the diner. "Y'all have to see this," he shouted. "It's snowing!"

Lola May let out a joyful cry and practically ran to the door. "I lived the first five years of my life in Michigan," she said as she passed Keaton's table. "I never stopped missing the snow."

He slowly stood and turned to Francesca. "I take it Austin doesn't see a lot of snow?"

"Hardly ever. What about London?"

"Very little, although it snowed on Christmas right before I moved here. Maybe it's a sign." Sparks zipped up and down her spine at the way he looked at her.

"We'd better go out with everyone," she whispered. "Wouldn't want to miss this."

"No indeed." He held out a hand. "Shall we?"

Swallowing back her nerves, she slipped her fingers into his. He held her hand gently, but she felt the contact all the way to her toes.

The cold air took her breath away as they exited the restaurant. "It's real," she whispered then giggled as she watched Lola May spin in a circle in the middle of the street.

Ciara and her friends were already halfway down the block, cheering and laughing as they walked in a tight group. The whole neighborhood had an otherworldly quality to it tonight. Residents and business owners from nearby buildings filed out into the street to take part in this rare occasion. A dozen heads tipped up to the sky, and Francesca's was one of them. She lifted her face and closed her eyes, loving the feel of the icy flurries melting on her skin.

Keaton interlaced their fingers and lifted her hand to his mouth, gently kissing her knuckles. "You are so gorgeous," he murmured.

Francesca's face heated in response to the compliment and she could almost feel the snowflakes sizzle as they landed on her.

"I don't want to make you uncomfortable," he told her. "But I can't not say it. You are the most beautiful woman I've ever met."

Maybe it was something about the rareness of a Texas snowfall, but a thrill of anticipation—as opposed to nerves—shot through her at his words. "Thank you." She went onto tiptoe to brush a quick kiss against his cheek. "I can't think of anyone I'd rather share this moment with than you."

Someone opened a window in the storefront next to Lola May's and a soft country ballad spilled out into the night.

"May I have this dance?" Keaton asked. When she nodded he spun her under his arm and then pulled her closer.

Francesca loved the feeling of his hand splayed across her back, the heat radiating off him warming her in the cold night air. They didn't speak for several minutes, only swayed under the streetlight. The rest of the neighborhood moved around them, but Francesca felt like she and Keaton were suspended in time, alone in their own intimate bubble.

The song ended and another—a fast-paced country anthem—took its place. Francesca and Keaton broke apart as Lola May walked over to them.

"It's sticking," she said, pure joy in her tone.

The street and sidewalk were clear, but snow lay like a thin, white blanket over the patch of grass in front of the apartment building a few doors down.

Francesca laughed. "This almost counts as a blizzard in Austin."

"I'm going to finish in the kitchen," Lola May told her. "I don't want to be driving home too late. People in Texas lose their ability to steer when the weather gets bad."

"I'll be in early tomorrow to help you prep," Francesca told her, and Lola May patted her shoulder before returning to the diner.

Already the flurries were coming down slower. "I think the blizzard is almost at an end," she said with a sigh.

Keaton leaned close to her. "It was fun while it lasted."

Fun.

Tonight had been fun.

Francesca felt a smile tug at the corners of her mouth. She had a momentary urge to chase after Ciara and reveal to her friend that Francesca hadn't totally forgotten how to have fun.

Instead she lifted her gaze to meet Keaton's light eyes and asked, "Would you like to go for coffee with me sometime?"

His eyes widened for a second and she quickly added, "I know you're busy with work and the Fortunes so—"

"I'd love to," he interrupted. "How about tomorrow? I can make time tomorrow." He let out a soft laugh. "I can make time whenever you want."

Oh. Well. That was something.

Her heart raced in her chest at his words. She was used to fitting in to other people's lives and schedules. But this man wanted to make time for her.

"I have an early class," she told him, "but I'll be free around eleven. Could you meet me on campus? We can take a tour, and I'll make you an unofficial Longhorn." She paused then added, "It will be fun."

"Sounds like it," he answered. "Eleven works. Text me where to meet you." Once again, he brought her hand to his lips and placed a gentlemanly kiss on her knuckles. "I'm looking forward to it."

"Me, too," she breathed then glanced over her shoulder. "I should go and help Lola May finish up."

Keaton nodded. "Until tomorrow then," he said and waited for the front door of the diner to close behind her before turning and heading down the sidewalk.

Francesca could hardly wait for tomorrow to arrive.

Keaton checked his watch. 10:45. He was standing at The Tower, the colloquial name given to the Main Building in the center of the University of Texas at Austin campus. It was only a short walk from the corner where he was supposed to meet Francesca in fifteen minutes. He didn't want to seem too eager and take the chance of making her nervous.

Her unexpected invitation to coffee had been the best thing to happen to him in as long as he could remember. It was still difficult to know exactly why spending time with the adorable waitress had so quickly become entwined with his happiness, but he didn't bother to pretend otherwise.

Maybe it was her unique combination of spunky

and shy that had taken hold of him. She was a breath of fresh air, someone who didn't want anything from him. Most of the women he'd known in London had been quite forward in their advances. As word spread about his connection to the Fortune family here in the States, he wasn't sure whom to trust. Coming from his simple background, he found it sometimes a challenge to sort out his newfound notoriety. Talking to a reporter like Ariana Lamonte was straightforward enough, but it was the new supposed friends that worried him. It was difficult to know what motivated them to make claims on his time.

He only wished Francesca would give him more of *her* time. She'd fit perfectly in his arms last night as they danced, and he'd wanted an excuse to keep her there even longer. Keaton had never been a patient man. Since a young age, he'd been driven to succeed in every aspect of his life, whether in sports or academics or, later, in his career. He could talk a bloody good game about not caring that he'd grown up without a father. Yet the absence of a male role model in his life had influenced the very fiber of his identity.

Francesca made him feel at peace. He didn't have to prove anything to her and could solely enjoy her company. He also knew his mother would like her work ethic and the fact that she didn't seem impressed by Keaton's famous family or his professional reputation. She genuinely wanted to know him. For once he felt like he might be ready to give a woman more of him than he was normally willing to offer.

Not too much, of course. He didn't want to lead her on by allowing her to believe he was the type to settle down. A woman like Francesca would make a fantastic wife and mother. Some man would be lucky to claim her as his own. As much as Keaton's gut tightened at the thought of another pair of arms holding Francesca, he also understood he could never be the man she needed.

He brushed aside the maudlin train of his thoughts. It was a coffee date, nothing more. And even if he was no one's knight in shining armor, they could still have a good time together. Francesca deserved some relaxation and fun more than anyone he'd ever known.

With another quick check of the time, he moved forward through the campus. Students with backpacks and messenger bags slung over their shoulders hurried along the path that cut through campus. Despite the snowfall last night, today was warm with the sun shining brightly from a cornflower blue sky. The dusting of flurries had melted away and left only damp green grass.

He saw Francesca before she noticed him. Her hair was down and it pulled him like a beacon through the clusters of students milling about between classes. She was talking to a young man wearing a ubiquitous flannel shirt and sporting a scraggly beard that seemed to be de rigueur for a certain hipster crowd. The guy said something that made Francesca laugh, and jealousy spiked within Keaton. His possessiveness was ridiculous when he had no claim on Francesca. But he wanted to be the one to coax a laugh out of her. There was so much more to the blonde beauty than some punk kid could appreciate.

He lengthened his stride, suddenly desperate to be at her side. She glanced over her shoulder, as if she could sense his approach. Her smile widened and she quickly excused herself from the conversation and turned to him.

"Hey," he said quietly when they were standing toe to toe. It took every ounce of willpower he had not to reach for her.

She giggled. "My mom always said 'hay is for horses.'"

He liked that she was teasing him. It meant her nerves weren't getting the best of her. He took a step back and bent forward into a deep bow. "Good afternoon, Ms. Harriman," he said, mimicking the stuffy accent of his upper class friends. "You look quite fine today."

"Jeepers," she murmured, patting her chest with her open palm. "You take my breath away when you talk like that."

"What's a jeeper?" he asked, straightening.

She laughed again. "It's just an expression. One that probably gives me away as an unsophisticated small-town girl at heart." She held up a hand when he would have argued. "Wait, let me try." She sank into a somewhat off-balance curtsy. "G'day, guvnor." Her British accent was atrocious and made him grin hugely. "Lovely weather we're havin'. Right then. Cheerio." She looked up at him through her lashes. "How'd I do?"

"You sound like you've spent too much time watching *Mary Poppins*," he told her with a chuckle.

She stuck out her tongue. "You can't do Texas and I'm horrible at a British accent. Looks like we're stuck being just who we are."

"Perfect for me," he agreed, and she inclined her

head toward a path that led away from the center of campus.

"The coffee shop is this way," she said and started to move in that direction.

He stopped her with a hand on her backpack. "Let me carry this for you."

"You don't have to."

"I want to," he said and noticed she blushed as she removed the backpack and handed it to him.

"I've never had anyone carry my books."

"I'm honored to be the first," he said and they walked together down the tree-lined path.

Chapter Six

As Francesca settled in at the table near the front window of the local coffee shop ten minutes later, she touched her well-worn backpack and tried to hide the smile that wanted to bloom at Keaton's thoughtfulness. She'd had trouble holding back a bark of hysterical laughter when he'd taken her backpack. For years, she'd schlepped duffel bags, equipment and instruments for Lou and his bandmates. Many times it had been Francesca loading up the tour bus while the boys had a few beers after a show with friends or various groupies.

Most of the guys had been grateful, but Lou had always acted like she should be honored to play the role of unofficial Sherpa. She'd discovered far too late that he'd taken advantage of the time when she was busy working to indulge in random hookups with women who came to the shows.

She was also embarrassed to admit how long it had been before the demise of their relationship that she and Lou had been intimate. Of course she'd been tested after discovering his infidelity, but the clean bill of health she'd received had only been a small comfort.

It hadn't changed the fact that she'd been a fool to let her heart lead when her head had been broadcasting warning signals for years.

She watched Keaton lean over the pastry case at the coffee shop favored by university students and couldn't help but notice how the three young coeds working the counter gaped at him. The man was sinfully handsome in his dark gray dress slacks and tailored shirt. As he moved, the fabric stretched across the hard planes of his back, the muscles bunching in a way that made her mouth go dry. Out of the corner of her eye, she saw one of the baristas bite her bottom lip.

Another kind of heat gripped her chest as she realized she was quickly getting in way over her head with the sexy Brit.

After Lou's betrayal, Francesca had sworn off men. At the same time she'd promised herself that when she was ready to dip her foot back into the dating pool, she'd pick a man better suited to her. Keaton was so far out of her league they weren't even playing the same sport.

But he'd carried her backpack. He'd called her beautiful.

She reminded herself that Keaton and Lou had nothing in common, and even if they had, it didn't matter. She was having *fun*. Nothing more.

"Why so serious?" She started as Keaton lowered himself into the seat across from her.

"Just thinking about a class project that's due next week," she lied.

"Tell me about it," he said and pushed a plate holding a muffin and two forks to the center of the table.

"I have to come up with a marketing plan for a business that has the goal of appealing to a broad section of the population. The idea is to develop PR and advertising that will attract a mix of demographics." That much at least was true. She had the assignment. She drew in a deep breath. "I've been working so many shifts at the diner that I haven't even settled on a business idea yet."

"Maybe you can use Austin Commons," he suggested. "If you want, I can put you in contact with the management company handling the grand opening for Phase One in a couple of months. It would be perfect, because the development is intended to attract a broad segment of the population. It could possibly lead to an internship or a job when you graduate."

She stared at him, not knowing quite how to respond.

"Or," he said, making a face, "you can tell me to shut my gob and bugger off."

"No, I don't mean that," she said quickly. "Although I don't exactly understand what you just said. But it's a really nice offer. I'm just not used to accepting help, you know? I've learned to take care of myself." She blew out a small breath. "And most of the people around me. It's the waitress in me. Sometimes I worry that even with a degree, I won't know how to do anything but look after people."

"I doubt that's true," he said, his blue eyes gentle. "But I understand. It's one of the most difficult things for me about being in America. There is no one in London to take care of my mum."

"Does she need a lot of help?"

He laughed. "Not according to her, and she'd kill me for giving you the impression that she does. She has a close group of mates. But who is going to fix a leaky faucet or repair the furnace when it's on the fritz?"

"I think that's why my mom always has a boyfriend hanging around," Francesca admitted. "She likes having someone to take care of her."

"My mother doesn't date."

The way he said it so matter-of-factly surprised Francesca. She sipped her coffee then asked, "Never?"

"She was really busy when I was a kid."

"And once you grew up?" She took a bite of muffin.

Keaton opened his mouth then shut it again. She waited for his answer, but he only shook his head.

"She's never met anyone?"

"I guess not," Keaton said and he sounded as surprised as she felt.

"Don't you think she wants a man in her life?"

"I… She isn't…" For once, Keaton seemed at a loss for words.

"It's difficult to think of our moms as people outside of who they are to us."

"She had her heart broken by Gerald Robinson," he said bluntly.

"Your father."

He shook his head as if he wanted to deny it even now. But after a moment he muttered, "Yes, my father. I don't think she ever recovered and now it's too late."

He looked so sad as he said the words. She wanted

to wrap her arms around his broad shoulders and give him the hug he obviously needed.

"Is she happy?" she asked instead.

"I thought so. I think so." He rubbed a hand over his jaw. "I bloody well hope so."

She reached for his hand and squeezed his fingers in hers. "You'd know if she wasn't. It's clear how close you are with her. I wish my mom and I were like that."

"You're not?" He traced his thumb over her skin, turning her insides to mush with just that simple touch.

"We're different." Francesca shrugged, unsure how to explain it. "She loves me, but she has a small view of the world and my place in it. I have a steady job at Lola May's, and my mom thinks I should be happy with that. She doesn't understand why I'm bothering with college. To her, I'm trying to be better than I am."

"Is there something wrong with that?" he asked.

Francesca blew out a breath. "I don't want you to get the wrong impression. My mom loves me. I think she's afraid I'll leave her behind if I have a degree and a career. I never knew my father, but he was someone my mom met when she was a hostess at a restaurant in a fancy hotel downtown. He travelled for business, but she didn't realize that he was already married with kids. Sometimes I think a part of her must have known, but she didn't want to admit it."

"I sometimes wonder how much my mum knew about Gerald Robinson during their short time together," Keaton said softly.

She nodded. "My father stopped seeing her before she even realized she was pregnant. He told her he couldn't take her seriously because she had no 'potential.'"

Keaton grimaced. "Ouch."

"Yeah, it hurt her badly," Francesca agreed. "She believed she wasn't good enough for him, and now she's afraid the same thing will happen with me. If I reach too far, life will beat me down for thinking I deserve more than what I already have. She acts like I'm trying to take after my father, which is crazy because I never knew him." She ran a trembling finger along the rim of her coffee cup, needing something to focus on to keep her emotions in check. "Of course, I'd never desert her or leave her behind. She's my mom."

"Are you curious about your dad?" Keaton covered her hand with his. The touch was warm and reassuring. "It sounds like he was never aware you existed."

"That's true," she admitted. "Once he walked away from my mom, she made the choice not to tell him about me. When I was younger I wanted a dad. It always seemed as though my friends who had both parents struggled less."

She looked past his shoulder at the line forming in front of the counter. So many times she'd stared at strangers, trying to find someone who resembled her. She'd had a strange, secret wish as a kid that she'd discover another girl with her same wild hair and that girl's father would take one look at Francesca and realize she was his daughter. She'd yearned for someone to claim her.

"It sounds silly, but the thing I wanted the most was to ride on my dad's shoulders. I always wondered what it would be like to see the world as the tallest person in the room." She pulled her hand away from his. "It would kill my mom if I ever tried to track him down. With all she sacrificed to raise me, I couldn't do that to her."

"I'm sorry you never had a set of shoulders to carry you."

She blinked back an unexpected rush of tears at the tenderness in his voice. Francesca thought she'd come to terms years ago with not having a father. It was something that set her apart from everyone else in her life.

Even her friends with divorced parents had some relationship with both their mother and father. Francesca's mom refused to speak the name of the man who had tossed her aside so carelessly. To share the same past with Keaton made their connection stronger than she could have imagined it being in such a short time. "Was it difficult for your mom when the Fortunes found you?"

He inclined his head and she saw his chest rise and fall as if the question had knocked the wind out of him.

"No one ever asked me that," he told her. "Ben was on such a mission to track down Gerald's illegitimate children once he discovered we were out there. I think the family understood it would be a shock for me, but I doubt they considered what the change would mean for my mother and our relationship."

"What did it mean?"

"It was an adjustment," he said, flashing a half smile that held no humor.

"Your lives would have been much different if you'd been Robinsons."

"Yes," he agreed, "but from that standpoint I understand why she never told me. Like your mother, I think mine was scared that she might lose me. The

Robinsons were a powerful family with money and connections even before the connection to the Fortunes was revealed. She could have never stopped Gerald if he'd decided he wanted me." He huffed out a bitter laugh. "Not that he wanted me. Unlike your father, mine knew I was on the way when he abandoned my mother."

"But you're in Austin now. You must have some contact with him?"

His hands fisted on the table and it was her turn to cover them with her own. This was certainly not the turn she'd expected the conversation to take on a first date, but she wouldn't change a thing about it. Something told her that despite his friends and his new Fortune family, Keaton felt as alone in the world as she did. She couldn't help her need to make him understand that wasn't how it had to be.

"Not if I can help it," he said through clenched teeth. "I've long ago come to terms with my father's actions, but I'll never forgive him for what he did to my mother."

Francesca didn't believe for a minute that Keaton had made peace with being rejected by Gerald Robinson, no matter what he claimed. "Then it's good you've become close with your half brothers and sisters," she said, wanting to erase the pain she saw hidden deep in his eyes.

"I'm grateful for that," he agreed. He smiled then and the pain was replaced with a brightness that lit up his face. "And that my time in Austin has led me to you."

Her breath hitched at the intensity in his gaze. How was she ever going to resist falling for this man?

* * *

The following Saturday afternoon, Keaton walked out of the barn at the ranch outside of Austin that his half brother Graham still managed on a part-time basis. He'd just finished grooming the mare he'd taken out for an hour-long trail ride.

He hadn't grown up riding horses—that had been a hobby of his wealthier friends with country estates in the pastoral countryside beyond London's city limits. But since getting to know Graham, who had close ties to the Galloping G ranch, Keaton had discovered a love for Western riding. He didn't assume that everyone in Texas was an avid horseman, but he wanted to ask Francesca if she'd like to come out for a ride with him.

Graham had given him access to the barn whenever he wanted and seemed glad for the horses to receive extra attention and exercise. Although he was devoted to the animals, Graham had a lot less time on his hands since being named CEO of Fortune Cosmetics last year. Graham had also found love with Sasha-Marie, the niece of the ranch's owner, when she'd returned to Austin last year.

Between the ranch, the cosmetics empire and Sasha and her two daughters to keep him busy, Keaton was surprised to find his half brother waiting for him in the driveway between the barn and the house.

"Have time for a beer?" Graham asked, holding up two bottles.

"Always," Keaton said and dusted his hands off on his jeans before taking one of the bottles. He tipped it back as Graham led him to two wooden rockers on the front porch of the ranch house. The cool liquid felt good on his parched throat. With the temperatures unseasonably warm for the past few days, it was hard to believe that he'd so recently danced with Francesca in the snow.

The sun was bright in the Texas sky, and he enjoyed the slight breeze that ruffled his hair.

"You need a hat," Graham commented as he dropped into one of the painted rocking chairs.

Keaton chuckled. "I'm British," he said. "We don't do cowboy hats."

"Give it some time." Graham pointed at Keaton's feet. "You've got boots. A hat to go with them can't be too far down the road."

Keaton crossed his ankles, glancing at the pointed tips of his new cowboy boots. He'd gotten them at a Western shop near his apartment, mainly because he hadn't packed anything that would be appropriate to wear riding.

"Besides," Graham added after taking a long pull on his beer, "you're only half-British."

Keaton smiled even as guilt stabbed through him. He appreciated how much his half siblings had done to welcome him into their fold, but the fact that he enjoyed being in Texas made him feel disloyal to his mother. She'd done so much for him and supported his decision to get to know the Fortunes, along with his mission to track down Gerald's other children. But he was all she had in life. After talking to Francesca, he had a clearer understanding of what his mother had sacrificed for him.

"The half that could kick your butt in a game of football," he said, saluting Graham with his beer.

"You're in Texas now, son." Graham purposefully

made his Texas drawl even more pronounced. "When you say football, you'd better be talking about Friday night lights, pigskin and cheerleaders."

"Soccer," Keaton amended with a smile.

"One of these days you can coach me on soccer and I'll show you how to throw a perfect spiral."

"Deal." Keaton took another drink. "Did your dad teach you how to play football?"

"Not so much," Graham answered. "He was away a lot. I didn't understand it then, but now I know why." He shook his head. "He was a busy man."

Keaton felt his gut twist. "I don't understand how he justified his affairs, even in his own mind. I guess we don't know for sure about the other illegitimate kids, but there was no question he was aware my mum was pregnant when he broke things off with her."

"I'm sorry," Graham said quietly. Third of the eight Robinson children by birth order, Graham was particularly easygoing. But Keaton could tell how much the news about his father's true identity and the ensuing fallout had affected him. Each one of Keaton's half siblings had apologized to him in one form or another since they'd first met.

"You have nothing to feel sorry for," he told Graham, echoing the same response he'd given the others. "If anything I should apologize to you. The Robinsons were simply your run-of-the-mill wildly successful, ridiculously wealthy family before all of this started."

"Yeah, right." Graham laughed. "We've all learned in the past year that nothing about our father is simple."

"I've been asked to sit down for an interview and profile story for *Weird Life Magazine* and their blog."

Graham raised a brow. "Ben mentioned that. Are you going to agree to it?"

"Yes," Keaton answered. "I talked to the reporter about my search for some of the others—" He broke off, cursing under his breath. "Others," he repeated after a moment, the word like acid on his tongue. "It sounds like I'm on the hunt for fugitives or alien life forms."

"You're searching for our brothers and sisters," Graham told him. "There's no shame for them or for you. All of us are at Dad's mercy in this. He won't talk about his mistresses or the children who have been born outside of his marriage to my mom. That's on him, Keaton. No one else."

"Thank you for saying that." Keaton took another draft of beer then set the bottle down on the wide-plank floor. "I understand it conceptually, but it doesn't hurt to hear someone else speak the words."

"Anytime you need it," Graham answered.

"About the article... Ariana Lamonte," Keaton said, "is the reporter doing the feature. She's going to make it clear in her article that there may be more Fortunes yet to be revealed. I've asked her not to speak specifically about how much Gerald or your mother might have known. My intention isn't to drag the family through the mud."

He saw Graham's jaw tighten even as he nodded. "I appreciate that, although I wouldn't blame you if it was."

"That's not going to help anyone."

Graham leaned forward, elbows on knees, and glanced over at Keaton. "Can I ask you a candid question?"

Keaton nodded. "By all means."

"Why *are* you trying to find these other Fortunes? I get Ben's motivations. He's always been the bold one, and as Dad's presumptive heir, he was shaken by what we learned last year. He felt it was his duty to find out the truth and track down you and whoever else is out there. In his heart, he wants to reunite the family." He shrugged. "But you have every reason to hate our father, yet you haven't done anything to make a claim on the family money or to publicly ruin his reputation." Graham tipped his head toward Keaton. "You could do both of those things without much effort, especially if you've got the attention of a reporter."

"I don't want anything from Gerald Robinson," Keaton confirmed. "But I do want to connect with people in the same situation as me. No one chooses to grow up without knowledge of who their father is. If Gerald has other children out there—"

"And we both know he does," Graham interrupted.

"They deserve to know," Keaton finished.

"What if they don't want to be a part of the Fortune family?"

"We'll cross that bridge when we come to it. Ben and I are making sure our research is thorough. Before we approach anyone, we need to be certain they are who we think they are. That's where Ariana can help."

Graham stared out over the front porch rails. Keaton followed his gaze and saw two horses nuzzling each other in the far pasture. "I don't want to be defined only by becoming a Fortune," he said after a moment. "But I can't deny it's changed who I am and how I think of myself. I hope it's changed me for the better, but that remains to be seen."

"You're a good man, Keaton."

"You, too, Graham." Keaton laughed softly. "I'm continually impressed with my brothers and sisters and the fully formed adults you are given who your father is and how he acted for so many years. Your mother must be an amazing woman."

Graham stood abruptly and shot Keaton a look he couldn't interpret. The tall rancher and newly minted head of a major corporation walked to the edge of the porch before turning. "I'm lucky, just like Wes and Ben are, to have found a truly amazing woman to share my life."

Keaton straightened from the rocker, thinking of Francesca. He was taking her out tonight and had planned the evening with the level of detail he'd use for his biggest client. Sharing coffee had been a lovely interlude and it still blew his mind how effortless it was to talk to her. But tonight was about blowing her mind and making her understand how truly special she was.

There was a fine line between wooing her and scaring her away, but he was willing to walk that line and give her a night out she wouldn't soon forget. It was clear she hadn't had enough people in her life who made her a priority. He was going to be the one to change that.

Chapter Seven

Francesca opened the door a little before seven to reveal Keaton standing on the other side, his hand raised as if he was about to knock.

She sucked in a breath as his blue gaze raked over her. He looked ten kinds of hot and sexy in a pair of black pants and an olive-green collared shirt.

"Hullo," he said slowly, looking into her eyes.

"I saw you park," she said, gesturing behind her to the picture window that looked out to the street in front of her building. "Not that I was staring…or waiting…or babbling."

"Take a breath, Francesca."

She drew air in and out of her lungs, trying—in vain—to calm her racing heart. "Why am I so nervous?" she asked, hysterical laughter rising up her throat. She swallowed it down and forced herself to smile. "I'm sorry I'm nervous. It makes me babble."

"You have no reason to be nervous," he said and pulled an arm from behind his back to reveal a bouquet of yellow roses. "Or to apologize. I like you being excited for me to arrive."

"Excited," she repeated dumbly. There were at least two dozen blooms in the massive bunch, each flower more vibrant than the next.

"These are for you." He handed her the bouquet. "I wasn't sure of your favorite but since yellow roses are synonymous with Texas, I thought you might enjoy them."

"You know that song was written about a slave girl," she said as she lifted the flowers to her nose, closing her eyes and inhaling deeply. "She was said to have distracted the Mexican general Santa Anna so that Sam Houston and his men could ride across the plains and have their victory at the battle of San Jacinto."

"Fascinating," Keaton murmured.

Francesca's eyes snapped open. "I'm still babbling," she muttered then took a step back into the apartment. "Please come in while I put these in water and try to get my brain working again."

She could barely make eye contact with him. Keaton Whitfield was handsome, smart and very successful. He could have any woman he wanted, and all Francesca could manage was to give him a history lesson on a famous Texas folk song. She was an idiot.

She took a vase from the cabinet, filled it with water and arranged the flowers as well as she could given that her fingers were trembling. Keaton took her hand as she turned back to him, tugging her closer.

"I like how your brain works," he said. "I like a lot of things about you."

He leaned in on the last words and his lips met hèrs. Francesca wasn't expecting the kiss, which left her no time to panic. She simply reacted to it, savoring the feel of his strong but gentle mouth against hers. He smelled like an intoxicating mix of mint and subtle cologne, and she had the craziest urge to press her nose into his neck.

Her eyes drifted closed instead, just as he ran his tongue across the seam of her lips. She felt the touch all the way down to her toes.

Too soon he pulled back. "I knew kissing you would be perfect," he whispered as he smoothed the pads of his thumbs over her cheeks.

"I don't have a lot of experience," she answered, "but don't you normally save the kiss for the end of the night?"

He laughed softly. "I couldn't wait. Do you feel less nervous now?"

She thought about the question for a moment then nodded.

"Right," he agreed. "Don't mistake me, Francesca. I have every intention of kissing you at the end of the evening." He pressed his lips to the sensitive place under her jaw. "I intend to kiss you as often as possible," he said against her skin. "You have no reason to be nervous." His lips brushed hers. "It will always be like this between us."

"Okay," she said, her voice coming out in a squeak. She cleared her throat. "But I'm a little worried."

He lifted his head, smoothed a curl away from her face. "About what?"

"Well," she said, biting down on her lower lip. "if you start the date like that, I'm not sure how you're going to top it."

Amusement flashed in his eyes. "Then we'd better start the evening so we can find out."

She grabbed her purse from the table, flipped off the lights and locked the door behind her. As they walked out onto the sidewalk, Keaton took her hand. She glanced toward Lola May's to see Ciara, Lola May and several of the regular customers staring out the front window.

"We have an audience." With his free hand, Keaton gave the group a small wave.

"I'm sorry," Francesca muttered. "Everyone is curious." They were probably trying to figure out what a man like Keaton saw in someone like her. At least she wasn't so inexperienced to say those words out loud.

"They care about you," he answered and she glanced over her shoulder toward the diner.

Ciara blew her a kiss, Lola May gave her the thumbs up and the two older men, who were truly like pseudo grandfathers, fist bumped each other then waved again.

Francesca smiled. Maybe Keaton was right and it wasn't that no one believed she was good enough for him. They were her family, and they wanted her to be happy.

Then she noticed where Keaton was leading her. "A limo?" she asked on a gasp.

"I thought it would be fun. Have you even been in one?"

She shook her head. Stinky tour buses, yes. Limousines, no.

The driver was waiting next to the back door and opened it as they approached. Francesca whispered her thanks as she climbed in, scooting forward on the plush leather seats.

Keaton settled next to her and took her hand. "I was so busy kissing you that I forgot to mention how beautiful you look." He traced his thumb in circles over the inside of her wrist, setting off a stream of tiny sparks across her skin. "You make that dress seem like something out of a fairy tale."

She'd chosen a beaded cocktail dress that indeed made her feel like a princess. It was deep purple color with a scooped neck and an empire waist. Between the diner and her classes, Francesca didn't have much need for fancy clothes. But Ciara had insisted on taking her shopping after her break up with Lou. Retail therapy, her friend had called it. Francesca had thrown out every band T-shirt and article of black clothing she owned. She associated the dark color with all the nights spent trying to hide herself backstage at Lou's gigs.

Ciara had encouraged her to buy an outfit that represented the new chapter in her life and who she wanted to be. As soon as Francesca had seen the flirty, youthful dress she'd known it was perfect. It had hung in her closet with the tags still on until tonight. Tonight with Keaton she was who she wanted to be. She felt like the best part of herself when she was with him.

He didn't expect her to change to accommodate his needs the way Lou had or try to limit her options so she wouldn't get hurt, like her mother sometimes did. Keaton helped her see that there was more to her than she gave herself credit for. Even if this magical night was the only one she had with him, she'd always remain grateful for that gift.

"This is better than a fairy tale," she said. "Because it's real."

"Yes, it is."

As the limousine wound through the streets of downtown Austin, Keaton told her about his visit to the ranch his half brother Graham still helped manage when time allowed. He seemed surprised that she didn't ride, but she explained that she'd spent her entire childhood near downtown. Austin wasn't as big as London, but there were plenty of non-cowboys living in the city.

"One of the few things my mom would tell me about my father," she said, leaning her head back against the soft leather of the limo's backseat, "was that he wore a cowboy hat when he stayed at the hotel." She picked at the hem of her dress. "She called it his 'damned hat.' I always thought maybe he had a ranch or some kind of horse property. I imagined that if I ever got to know him, he'd teach me how to ride."

"I'll teach you," he offered.

"I'd like that," she answered with a smile, both because she loved the idea of being on horseback and because it meant Keaton was thinking of spending time with her beyond tonight. She already knew she wanted more.

The limo came to a stop in front of a charming, redbrick building tucked into a quiet street west of downtown. Francesca glanced out the window and sucked in a breath. "Do you know where we are? This is Il Fontaine."

Keaton chuckled. "Who do you think gave the driver directions? They're expecting us."

The door to the limo opened and he started to move toward it, but she grabbed his arm. "This is the top-rated restaurant in the city," she said. "It takes months to get a reservation here."

He flashed a small smile. "One of the partners at the firm designed the space. He made a call for me."

"It's super expensive," she said on a hiss of breath. "We can do something less—"

"We're having dinner at Il Fontaine," he said calmly. "For the record, I'd really like to punch the man who made you believe you don't deserve the best of everything."

She opened her mouth to argue then snapped it shut when tears pricked the back of her eyes. She *did* believe she wasn't deserving of the best. She wanted to change that. Not that she needed five-star dinner dates, but the fact that Keaton wanted her to experience this meant a lot to her. She wished it was as easy as blaming Lou the Louse, but Francesca had allowed herself to be made to feel small. She hadn't expected someone to care if she felt differently.

She scooted toward Keaton and placed a kiss on his cheek. "Thank you for tonight."

He tapped a finger on the tip of her nose. "The night has barely started."

"It's like the kiss," she answered. "Between you and me, it's bound to be perfect."

The evening made Keaton want to experience everything through her eyes. In London, between his work and the social circles in which he now traveled, he'd been to countless formal dinners. Nothing about an exclusive reservation at a trendy restaurant, a menu of elaborate food prepared by a famous chef or an expensive bottle of wine impressed him.

But it all felt new with Francesca. Thanks to the partner at his firm, he'd been able to book Il Fontaine's private dining room on the third floor of the building. They sat at a table for two, the space lit by dozens of candles. The room boasted an impressive view of downtown Austin, and it felt like they were a world away from everyday life. It was a feeling Keaton wanted to capture and hold.

He'd arranged for an eight-course tasting menu selected by the chef because he wanted to concentrate on Francesca. She'd been delighted by every new plate brought to their table, from the butternut squash soup they'd started with to the brie in crispy phyllo dough with candied pecans to the pan-seared scallops that had been served as the main course.

He watched her sip her third glass of wine as the waiter set the dessert course on the table. It was a dark-chocolate flourless cake with an espresso mousse, fresh berries and whipped cream topping it.

"It's almost too beautiful to eat," Francesca murmured.

Not nearly as beautiful as you, Keaton wanted to tell her. He had no skill with flowery compliments or poetry but looking at Francesca made him understand how generations of love-struck poets had been inspired to place pen to paper. Her eyes sparkled in the candlelight and her wild mane of hair cascaded over her shoulders in a way that made him wonder what it would look like spread across his pillow. Heat pooled low in his belly at the mental image of this woman curled around him in bed.

"I've got to snap a picture to show Ciara," she said when they were alone again. She pulled out her phone and snapped a photo of her dessert. "Does this make me seem like a total bumpkin? I bet you're used to being served food that looks like art." She made a face. "You must think the homestyle cooking at Lola May's is so ordinary in comparison."

"I choose to eat at Lola May's almost every day," he said with a chuckle. "Clearly it appeals to me." He waited until she met his gaze then added, "But it isn't only the food that keeps me coming back."

"I noticed you the first time you walked into the restaurant," she said quietly. She ducked her head and color rushed to her cheeks, making him understand she hadn't meant to admit as much. A surprising zing of happiness shot through him in response.

"That's not true," he protested. "You wouldn't even make eye contact for the first week I came in."

She arched a brow. "You were wearing charcoal-gray trousers, a dark blue shirt and a striped tie. You sat at the counter and ordered a cheeseburger and fries. Lola May waited on you and, within minutes, she was giggling like a schoolgirl at whatever you were saying."

"She'd told me the ages of her kids and I commented that she must have had them when she was just a toddler because she looks so young."

Francesca snorted then raised her fingers to her mouth. "Sorry," she mumbled through her fingers. "But that's laying it on a little thick, wouldn't you say?"

"All I know is she cut me the first slice of the apple pie she'd baked that morning."

"You're too charming for your own good," she answered, pointing a finger at him. "Do you always get what you want?"

He leaned across the table toward her. "Always."

She reached for her wineglass, but knocked it with her fingers instead. Before either of them could react, the delicate piece of stemware tipped onto its side, golden liquid spilling across the table.

Keaton jumped up from his seat in time to miss the wine dripping into his lap. Grabbing the glass, Francesca let out a little yelp of embarrassment. "I'm so sorry," she said, using her napkin to blot at the white table cloth. "Why am I so klutzy around you?"

"If I didn't know better, Ms. Harriman," he said with a wink, "I'd think you wanted me to take off my pants."

He regretted the words as soon as they were out of his mouth. Instead of a delicate blush, her cheeks flamed bright pink and her mouth dropped open as if he'd just accused her of running naked through the center of town.

"I—I don't…" she stammered.

"It was a joke, Francesca." He came around the table and reached for her hand. "A bad one, and I'm sorry for it."

Her gaze fell to the floor. "I know I'm nothing like the women you're used to taking out for a dinner date."

"And I couldn't be more grateful," he said.

"You know I have a reputation for never dropping anything at the restaurant?" She moved to sit back down. He let her but kept hold of her hand. He couldn't get enough of touching her, even so innocently. "Since I moved back to Austin, I haven't broken a single plate or glass. It's been almost two years."

"Your record stands," he told her. "The wineglass is still intact, and the plate of pot pie had a soft landing in my lap."

She rolled her eyes. "You need to stop making me nervous."

He laughed at the annoyance in her command. "I like that I have an effect on you." With his free hand, he scooped up a spoonful of dessert and held it out to her. She bit down on her lower lip then opened her mouth for the bite. It was pure pleasure to watch her eyes drift close as a soft moan escaped her mouth.

"That is the best thing I've ever put in my mouth," she whispered.

He couldn't agree more, but this time he was smart enough to keep his mouth shut.

An hour later the limo pulled to a stop in front of Lola May's.

The restaurant was dark, as were the windows in her apartment above the diner. Francesca climbed out when the driver opened the door, her entire body humming with need. Keaton had tucked her into his side on the ride home, his fingers tracing light patterns over the bare skin of her leg just under the hem of her dress.

She'd asked him to tell her about growing up in London, and he'd obliged with funny stories about the mischief he'd made at school and playing in his neighborhood soccer club. But between the slight buzz she felt from the wine and her awareness of him, she could barely remember a thing he said.

"I'll walk you to your door," he murmured into her ear, his hand coming to rest low on her back.

"Thanks," she answered because she didn't trust herself to say more. All of the other thoughts running through her head sounded like "stay the night" and she'd already embarrassed herself enough for one evening.

She tripped a little bit at the top of the stairs and blamed the stupid heels she wasn't used to wearing. She hadn't had *that* much to drink, had she?

Keaton caught her and pulled her close. Her back pressed to his chest, she was once again enveloped in his warmth and the spicy scent of him. The combination did crazy things to her senses. She'd never had this reaction to any man, not Lou even in the early days of their relationship and not with any of the customers who'd flirted with her over the years at Lola May's. Her body had a mind of its own when it came to Keaton, and she was having a difficult time remembering why she'd ever had doubts about this handsome, sexy Brit.

"Are you okay now, luv?" he asked, his voice a deep rumble that she was coming to crave as much as chocolate.

She let out a little sigh, tempted to snuggle closer to him. She wanted to turn into him and press her nose to the base of his throat. Her whole body ached to have his hands on her, to tip up her chin and kiss him. Instead, she jerked away, propelling herself the two steps forward to her door. There was no way she was going to maul Keaton in the hallway outside her tiny apartment. She placed her palms on the smooth wood to ground herself then reached into her purse for her key.

"I'm fine," she muttered, jabbing the key into the lock. Once it clicked open, she turned to face Keaton.

He'd stepped toward her and reached out a hand to smooth her hair away from her face. "I had a great time tonight." He lifted his arms to hold on to the top of the doorframe and her mouth went dry at the way his muscles tightened under the crisp fabric of his shirt.

"Me, too," she whispered, swaying closer to him. "Thank you for dinner. I've never experienced anything like that. I can now check off a limo ride from my bucket list."

One side of his mouth pulled up into an irresistible smile. "What else is on your bucket list?"

You.

She swallowed back the word. How many women had thrown themselves at Keaton? She refused to add her name to what she imagined was a long list.

"Rock climbing," she answered. "Scuba diving. Paris."

"Good to know," he said and bent until their lips almost touched. "If I had my way, Francesca, I'd make all your wishes come true."

I wish you would kiss me, she thought, and like magic, his mouth brushed over hers. The kiss was gentle and sweet, an exploration with a hint of something more.

She wanted the something more.

She wound her arms around his neck and went up on tiptoe, pressing her body against his. He released the doorframe and lowered his hands to her waist, spanning her curves with his fingers. He was hard in the places she was soft, and she reveled in the feel of him. Their contrasting backgrounds might make her nervous most of the time, but in this case their differences blended to make them a perfect fit.

Perfect.

There was no other way to describe how she felt in his arms. Her lips parted, a silent invitation. When he took it, sliding his tongue into her mouth, she wasn't sure if the groan of pleasure she heard came from him or her. Either way, it ignited a fire inside her and suddenly she couldn't get enough of him. The kiss deepened, all of her senses going crazy as his hands slid down her back and over her hips to pull her even closer.

She sucked in a breath as her belly pressed against the evidence of his arousal. It gave her a strange and gratifying sense of power to know that this man wanted her.

Almost immediately he pushed away and took a step back into the hallway. She heard him mutter a curse under his breath and her fingers went to her lips. She could still feel the imprint of his mouth on hers, and her whole body protested the distance between them.

When he met her gaze, he flashed an apologetic smile. "Well, then," he said, clearing his throat. "That was unexpected."

Unexpected. Francesca's heart sank. There were other words she was thinking of—amazing, mind-blowing, awesome. Unexpected was a bit of a letdown, to say the least.

"A lovely surprise," Keaton whispered and she wondered what he was reading in her eyes. He reached for her hand. "A perfect beginning and a perfect end. Talk about sweet dreams."

Lovely and perfect were an improvement. Francesca studied him, hoping he wasn't merely trying to soothe her bruised pride.

His gaze was gentle. "I should go now," he told her, placing a tender kiss on each of her knuckles. "Before I find it impossible to leave."

She wanted to believe he meant that, almost as much as she wanted to ask him to stay. "Thank you again," she said instead. "It really was a perfect evening."

He studied her for a moment, his gaze so intense it felt as if he was searching for an answer to a question he wasn't even sure how to ask.

Then he smiled, the look he gave her turning playfully charming, and just like that, the moment was over.

"I'll talk to you soon," he said and disappeared down the stairs.

Francesca walked into her apartment and kicked off the shoes she knew would leave a blister on her feet. She inched to the window and peeked out from behind the curtains. Just before he got back into the limo, Keaton glanced up at her apartment. There was no way he could see her, but it felt like he was looking directly at her.

That man could make her melt with once glance.

She was in big trouble.

Chapter Eight

"A man like that is trouble for a girl like you."

Francesca tried to shrug off the words her mother spoke the next morning. She wasn't having any more luck ignoring the verbal jab than she was in getting rid of her massive headache.

Three glasses of wine with dinner and now she had a hangover the size of Houston. When had she become such a lightweight?

She sighed and took another drink of the soda she'd ordered at her favorite drive-thru restaurant on the way to her mom's small condo. The hamburger and fries sat untouched on the kitchen table, but she'd get to those as soon as her stomach settled. The truth was she'd never been a drinker. Her role had always been designated driver or caregiver to Lou and his band-mates when they overindulged. Now she was the one who was paying the price for a night of overdoing it.

"He's a nice guy," she said to her mom, who was wiping down the counters as they spoke. "We have fun together."

"What could you possibly have in common with a Fortune?" Paige Harriman turned and rested one hand on her hip. "You come from two different worlds."

"Not that different," Francesca argued, wishing she hadn't even mentioned her date with Keaton. "He only found out last year that Gerald Robinson was his father. Even Gerald's other kids didn't know their dad was really Jerome Fortune."

Her mother's eyes rolled to the ceiling. "Rich people issues," she said dismissively. "Or what is it they call those now? First-world problems."

Francesca unwrapped the hamburger and nibbled the edge of the bun. "Keaton was raised by a single mom, too. He didn't have a relationship with his dad, and his mom worked hard to take care of him." She raised her gaze to her mother's. "Just like you."

"Sometimes I think we raised each other, Frannie." Her mom dropped the sponge into the sink and came to sit across from her at the table. "You were more mature than me even when you were a girl."

"That's not true," Francesca answered, although in many ways it had been her reality. Her mother had good intentions, but she'd let emotions rule most of the decisions she made and not always with the best outcome.

"Trust me on this, sweetie." Paige snagged one of the fries. "We're not the same as people like the Fortunes. We're simple, you know? Working class. I thought I could make myself into someone different. I believed loving a man was enough to change my life. Look at where that got me."

Francesca had just taken another bite of hamburger, and it seemed to turn to sawdust in her mouth. She didn't want to hear how dating Keaton was going to set her up for the same type of heartache her mom had endured.

"Don't get upset," her mother told her. "I don't mean you. You're the best thing that ever happened to me. But our lives could have been different if I'd made better choices. I wasn't good enough for a man like your father."

"He was married," Francesca said. "You had an affair with a married man, who already had a wife and kids. It's different, Mom."

Paige shrugged. "He said he loved me. He let me believe we would be together."

"I've been on two dates with Keaton. He hasn't made any promises, and I don't expect him to. It's just *fun.*" She wasn't sure which one of them she was trying to convince.

Her mother wagged a finger in the air. "I recognize that look in your eyes. You're falling for him, and we both know you give your heart too easily."

Francesca opened her mouth to argue then snapped it shut again. She *was* falling for Keaton, even after knowing him for such a short time. It was part of the reason she'd kept her distance when he'd first come into Lola May's. She'd felt a connection to him even before they'd officially met. Now that she knew he was sweet and funny in addition to being hot as the Texas plains in August, she was pretty much a goner.

Maybe that's why she'd tried to have her wicked way with him last night.

Heat rose to her cheeks at the thought of the way she'd deepened the kiss then practically mounted him when he'd obviously been trying to keep things casual. He was a gentleman, and she'd been a sloppy, drunken floozy.

"I'm not going to fall for him," she told her mother, wanting to believe she had the willpower to keep her heart out of the equation.

"You need to stick to someone who's more like you." Paige took another fry then added, "I saw Cowbell on one of the late night shows last night. They were the musical guest, and Lou sounded great."

"It's still the worst band name in the history of band names," Francesca muttered. "And if you remember, Lou cheated on me. Repeatedly. If you're insinuating that he was the one that got away, you're wrong. I should have kicked him to the curb long before I did."

"I'm saying you two come from the same place. You had a lot in common."

A bitter laugh bubbled up in Francesca's throat. "Mom, the only thing Lou and I had in common is that we both loved him."

"He made a mistake," her mother argued.

"More than one."

"He texted me last week."

Francesca choked on the sip of soda she'd just taken. "Why didn't you tell me?"

Paige shrugged. "I knew you'd be upset. He asked about you."

"Mom, don't text him. Don't talk to him. Lou and I broke up. I don't want anything to do with him."

"He still cares about you."

"Probably because he can't find anyone to do his laundry while he's on tour."

"You meant more to him than that."

"Right," Francesca agreed. "I made coffee every morning, too."

"You and Lou have a history together. You come from similar backgrounds. His band is breaking out, Frannie. If you're looking for a man to take care of you financially, he's just as good of a bet as your Fortune."

Francesca gripped the edge of the kitchen table until her knuckles turned white. "I'm not," she said through clenched teeth, "looking for a man to take care of me. I've got a job, Mom. I'm getting a college degree. I have every intention of supporting myself."

"I'm not trying to ruffle your feathers," her mom replied. "But it's hard making your way in the world alone. I know. I want what's best for you."

"And you think being with a man who cheats is the best I can do?"

"Don't put words in my mouth. Just go into this relationship with Keaton with your eyes open."

"We've been on *two* dates," Francesca shouted.

Paige crossed her arms over her chest. "You know what men expect on the third."

Francesca stood up from the table so fast she knocked over her chair. She shoved the barely eaten hamburger, fries and the empty soda cup into the paper bag. "I'm not having this conversation."

"I'm looking out for you," her mother said, a slight catch in her voice. She stood, wrapping her arms tightly around herself. "Please don't go away mad. I love when you visit, Frannie. Let's watch a show. I

DVRed some totally cheesy reality TV dating shows this week." Tears began to pool in her eyes.

Her mother had always been a crier, and Francesca was a sucker for tears. "I'm sorry, Mom," she said as she righted the chair and threw her garbage into the trash can under the sink. "I know you worry. I'm going to be careful with Keaton." She washed her hands, dried them on a towel then turned and gave her mother a hug. "But please don't talk to Lou."

"I won't." Her mother sniffed then hugged her back. "I know you can take care of yourself, and I'm so proud of you. You're smart and beautiful and you deserve the best life has to offer. That's all I want for you. I want you to feel special and loved. Choose a man who can love you like that, Frannie."

"I will," Francesca answered, although she wasn't sure she'd recognize that kind of love. Could Keaton be that man for her? It was silly to even consider it. They'd had two dates and whatever emotional bond she felt toward him, he'd made it clear that he was just having fun.

"Let's check out *Dating in the Wild*," her mother said as she stepped into the living room.

Francesca followed. Her relationship with her mother might not be perfect, but she knew her mom's intentions were good.

Even if Keaton was completely turned off by her behavior last night, Francesca had a full life and she could return to how things were before she'd met him.

Even if the thought of it made her heart ache.

Keaton's mood was as dark as the stormy sky over the city when he walked into Lola May's Monday evening. He'd had a frustrating day of fruitless searching for leads on one of Gerald's potential offspring. The information he had on the Frenchman tracking down a possible sibling seemed reliable, but he couldn't seem to get in touch with the man.

Then the general contractor on the Austin Commons project had run into an issue with one of his subcontractors. The stone they'd special ordered for the office space on the south side of the building was on backorder for at least a month, which would put the rest of that segment of the project on hold for six weeks or more. The mason they'd planned to use wasn't available past the middle of February, and it would derail the schedule for the rest of the building if he couldn't find someone to replace the master stone craftsman.

But the worst part of his day—the part that had him craving a stiff drink instead of the iced tea he'd get at Lola May's—was the fact that he'd texted Francesca this morning and only received a generic one-word response from her. Maybe he'd been an idiot to expect more after their last date, but he wanted it. One of the most difficult things he'd done in his life had been to walk away from Francesca last night when she'd been so clearly racked with the same need that gripped him every time he was near her.

She'd looked so beautiful standing in the doorway of her apartment, her blond hair cascading over her shoulders and her lips pink and swollen from his kisses. But even though she'd seemed interested in taking things further, he also realized she'd had too much to drink. He had no intention of taking advantage of her.

He hadn't wanted to scare her off with his kisses,

which it seemed was exactly what he'd done. His gaze immediately darted to the corner booth where he was used to seeing her study. A couple he didn't recognize occupied it tonight, sending a little pang of disappointment through him.

Lola May waved him over to the counter and he smiled, surreptitiously scanning the rest of the diner as he approached.

"Good evening," he said, sliding onto an empty stool. "I'll have—"

"She's in the back," Lola May told him. "My office is past the stockroom through the kitchen."

He didn't bother to pretend he didn't understand who she was talking about. "I'm not sure she wants to see me."

"Are you joking?" The older woman chuckled. "Honey, that accent of yours makes you sound real smart, but sometimes I wonder if you've got as many rocks for brains as the other guys sniffing around our girl."

"What other guys?" Keaton asked, his shoulders stiffening.

"Just about every man who walks through that door and gets a look at her. Francesca isn't a woman who blends into a crowd."

"I realize that, but—"

"Don't worry." Lola May placed a hand on Keaton's sleeve. "She hasn't given anyone the time of day for ages." She gently squeezed his arm. "Until you. She's been a bundle of nerves all night wondering when you'd come in, so I finally sent her to my office so she could concentrate on her schoolwork. That girl has a future beyond this diner, and I'm going to make sure she doesn't jeopardize it." She leaned in closer. "Not for anyone."

"I'm not a threat to her future." Keaton bristled at the suggestion, even as an uncomfortable feeling crawled across his back, like an itch he couldn't quite reach. He might not be a threat, but he also couldn't offer Francesca what she needed or deserved. He wasn't built for love, not after all he'd seen and experienced in his life. He shook his head, realizing he was getting ahead of himself. They'd only had two dates. It was far too early to worry about the future. "I want to make her happy."

Lola May studied him for a few moments then nodded. "We've got a roast chicken special tonight. You go check on Francesca and I'll bring your food to you when it's ready. I'll add a slice of fresh-baked lemon meringue pie to the order. Now get goin'."

Having been raised by his mother and her gaggle of nosy, overinvolved friends, Keaton was used to bossy women. Hearing Lola May tell him how to live his life didn't bother him in the least. In fact, it was one of the things that made this restaurant feel like home. Grinning, he stood from the counter and leaned forward to give her a quick kiss on the cheek.

"You keep that up," she said with a wink, "and I may keep you for myself."

As he walked toward the back of the diner, he could feel the eyes of the other customers on him. A waitress he recognized as Francesca's roommate gave him a thumbs-up sign and one of the old men who was a regular at the diner clapped him on the back.

"Good luck, son," the man told him. "Frannie's a keeper."

Did everyone know his business? Keaton threw a glance over his shoulder at Lola May, who shrugged as if to say "Deal with it, buddy."

He'd never liked being fodder for the gossip mill among his social circle in London. Yet the attention from the diner regulars didn't bother him as much as he would have expected. Francesca was worth having his personal life on display.

One of the guys working the kitchen's grill waved as if he'd been expecting him. The second cook did some aggressive chopping, his gaze trained on Keaton the whole time he wielded the knife.

The scene almost made him smile. He'd never been put on notice with a woman before, and he was glad Francesca had so many people looking out for her.

The door to Lola May's office was half-open, and he could see Francesca at the desk. Her back was to him as her fingers flew across the keyboard of her laptop. The room was tiny, no more than a converted supply closet. Bookshelves filled with binders lined one wall, and a massive metal file cabinet was lodged in the corner.

He knocked softly on the door and she whirled around in her chair.

"Hey," she said on a shallow breath.

"Hullo, Francesca. Do you have time for a study break?"

"Of course." She flipped closed the laptop and gestured to the chair across from the desk. "It's nice to see you."

Nice.

He didn't want nice from this woman, but he smiled.

"How was the rest of your weekend?"

FREE Merchandise and a Cash Reward† are 'in the Cards' for you!

Dear Reader,

We're giving away FREE MERCHANDISE and a CASH REWARD!

Seriously, we'd like to reward you for reading this novel by giving you **FREE MERCHANDISE** worth over $20 retail plus a CASH REWARD! And no purchase is necessary!

You see the Jack of Hearts sticker above? Paste that sticker in the box on the Free Merchandise Voucher inside. Return the Voucher today... and we'll send you Free Merchandise plus a Cash Reward!

Thanks again for reading one of our novels—and enjoy your Free Merchandise and Cash Reward with our compliments!

Pam Powers

Pam Powers

P.S. Look inside to see what Free Merchandise is **"in the cards"** for you!

We'd like to send you two free books like the one you are enjoying now. Your two books have a combined price of over $10 retail, but they are yours to keep absolutely FREE! We'll even send you 2 wonderful surprise gifts and a Cash Reward†. You can't lose!

REMEMBER: Your Free Merchandise, consisting of **2 Free Books** and **2 Free Gifts**, is worth over $20 retail! Plus we'll send you a **Cash Reward** (it's a dollar) which is really the icing on the cake because it's in addition to your FREE Merchandise! No purchase is necessary, so please send for your Free Merchandise today.

Get TWO FREE GIFTS!
We'll also send you 2 wonderful FREE GIFTS (worth about $10 retail), in addition to your 2 Free books and Cash Reward!

Visit us at:
www.ReaderService.com

Books received may not be as shown.

YOUR FREE MERCHANDISE INCLUDES...
2 FREE Books **AND** 2 FREE Mystery Gifts
PLUS you'll get a Cash Reward†

FREE MERCHANDISE VOUCHER

2 FREE BOOKS and **2 FREE GIFTS**

Please send my Free Merchandise, consisting of **2 Free Books** and **2 Free Mystery Gifts** PLUS my **Cash Reward**. I understand that I am under no obligation to buy anything, as explained on the back of this card.

235/335 HDL GLWM

Please Print

FIRST NAME

LAST NAME

ADDRESS

APT.#   CITY

STATE/PROV.   ZIP/POSTAL CODE

NO PURCHASE NECESSARY!

SE-N16-FMC15

▼ Detach card and mail today. No stamp needed. ▼

© 2016 HARLEQUIN ENTERPRISES LIMITED.® and ™ are trademarks owned and used by the trademark owner and/or its licensee. Printed in the U.S.A.

A rush of color stained her cheeks. "Fine."

Fine was worse than nice as far as Keaton was concerned.

"Did you have a relaxing Sunday?"

She nodded. "I spent the afternoon with my mom."

"That's…uh…nice." He couldn't figure out how to pull the conversation out of the tailspin it was in. It was like they were strangers again with so many awkward pauses and so much small talk between them.

"Um, Keaton…" Her gaze flitted to his, then skittered away.

He shifted in the chair. "Yes, Francesca?"

"I think I owe you an apology." Her voice was so soft he had to lean forward to make out her words.

"I doubt that," he answered, "but tell me why you think so."

"It probably makes me sound like a ninny, but I don't usually drink more than a glass of wine in a night."

He chuckled, unable to stop himself. Her delicate brows drew together and he immediately held up his hands, palms out. "I'm sorry. I've never heard anyone except my mum actually use the word *ninny*."

She made a face. "Well, at least you know what it means. Anyway, I think I drank a little too much on Saturday night."

"We shared one bottle of wine," he clarified. "Not quite a wild bender."

"Maybe not for you. But it was more than I'm used to."

"I take it you were feeling a bit tore up Sunday morning?"

"If that means I had a hangover, then yes," she admitted. "But I'm more concerned with my behavior Saturday night. I tried to take advantage of you. I'm sorry if I made you uncomfortable."

Bloody hell.

Keaton stared at her for longer than was polite, not sure how to respond. He'd been damned uncomfortable at the end of the date, but only because he'd forced himself to pull away from her when all he'd wanted was to sweep her into his arms and carry her to bed.

And she was apologizing for being too forward?

In all his days Keaton had never craved a woman the way he did Francesca. He'd tried to take things slow so as not to spook her, but to know that she might desire him with the same sort of intensity made a strange kind of peace descend over him. She wasn't blowing him off as he'd feared. He had to resist the urge to pump his fist in the air.

"Now I've made things more awkward." She practically leaped from her chair like she was about to bolt from the room.

He reached for her, grabbing her wrist and tugging her into his lap.

She gave a little "oof" then lifted her hands to his chest. He wasn't sure whether she was holding on or pushing him away so he looped his arms around her waist.

"We need to begin this conversation again," he said gently and kissed the tip of her nose. "Hullo, Francesca." He brushed his lips across her cheek. "I hope you enjoyed the rest of your weekend." He trailed his mouth over her jaw. "Leaving you," he whispered then gently sucked her earlobe into his mouth, "was pure torture for me. I've thought about you every moment since then."

She let out a little gasp, whether from his words or his touch he couldn't tell. He also didn't care.

"I've been counting the minutes until I could see you again." He pulled back so their gazes met. "Until I could kiss you again." Tilting his head, he captured her mouth, not bothering with gentle or slow. He showed her exactly how much he'd missed her.

After a few minutes, she broke the connection. Looking at him tentatively she asked, "So you didn't mind me attacking you?"

"If that was an attack," he said, nipping at the corner of her mouth. "you can assault me any day. Is that why I received a generic response to my text?"

"I was embarrassed. I know you were trying to take things slow and—"

"Because I respect you," he told her. "I don't want you to think I'm only interested in you physically." He tapped a fingertip on her forehead. "I'm fascinated by the way your mind works and..." He reached for her hand then pressed her palm to her chest, covering her hand with his. "I'm captivated by the way you care about the people in your life. Make no mistake, I want you. But even more, I want to get to know you. That's why I'm not rushing things." He could feel her heart thrumming and the knowledge of how he affected her made him want to share more of himself. More than he had with anyone before. "You mean the world to me, and I'll wait as long as it takes for this to be right for both of us. Every moment we have together is precious. I wouldn't change a thing about us, Francesca. You are too important to me."

Chapter Nine

Francesca's heart soared at Keaton's words.

"You're important to me, too," she said softly.

"So tell me about what you're so intently studying tonight," he told her.

Francesca paused before answering. Although both Lola May and Ciara supported her goal of getting her college degree, neither one of them seemed to care about the details of her course work. She rarely talked about school with her mother, either, because her mom didn't place much value on higher education. Other than her friends from school, there wasn't anyone else she could talk to about her studies. But Keaton asked her questions about her courses every time they were together and really seemed to care about the answers. It was one more way he was slowly slipping past her defenses.

"I'm working on my ad campaign project." She

took a breath then rested her head against his shoulder. "Thank you for putting me in touch with the marketing director at Austin Commons. She's been a huge help by giving me access to some of their initial planning. She likes that I have a history with the neighborhood and how my project focuses on the balance of bringing new customers to the area and serving the current community. We have a meeting set up later this week to discuss my initial concepts."

"Sounds like a good match," he said.

"I'm definitely more confident in marketing than in my accounting class." She lifted her head and flashed him a grin. "But I forgot to tell you, I got my grade back Friday on the test. A ninety-four."

"Congratulations," he said, kissing her again. "You worked hard for that A."

"With your help."

"I was happy to give it."

She glanced behind her at the open door. "Did you come in for dinner?"

"I came in to see you," he told her. "But, yes, I'm having dinner, as well. Lola May said she'd bring it to me here."

"Oh, no." She scrambled out of his lap, smoothing her shirt down over her hips. "We've got to get out there now."

He chuckled. "You do realize we're both adults and she's not your mother?"

"Well, yes," she answered, grabbing her laptop from the desk. "But Lola May is the biggest gossip in the neighborhood. If she caught me in your lap, everyone in the diner would know in minutes. Heck, she'd probably post it in the neighborhood newsletter."

"Would that be so bad?" he asked as he stood. "Based on everyone's reaction to me coming back here to find you, we aren't a huge secret."

She'd made it as far as the doorway and turned to face him. "Austin is a big city but this neighborhood functions like a small town. I don't mind people knowing, but I'm not looking to be the topic of conversation for anyone." She rose up on tiptoe to kiss him. "As far as I'm concerned, this is between us."

She wasn't certain, but Keaton seemed to let out a relieved breath at her words. "I like the sound of that," he said. "I like everything about you, Francesca."

"Right back at you." She kissed him again then headed through the kitchen. She stopped long enough to introduce Keaton to Richard and his brother, Jon, the two cooks who ran the kitchen at Lola May's. The men had worked at the diner since she'd started as a waitress in high school. Over the years they'd become like surrogate uncles to her. In a strange way she wanted them to approve of Keaton.

It only took a few minutes before Richard invited Keaton to go four-wheeling with them the following weekend. For a suave Brit who favored expensive clothes and designer shoes, Keaton had remarkable skill at convincing people he was just a regular guy. She wasn't sure if the two salt-of-the-earth kitchen workers knew about his connection to the Fortunes, but now that they'd accepted him it wouldn't matter. Keaton was in as far as they were concerned. Francesca couldn't help but compare that to how Richard and Jon had treated Lou the Louse. In all the years he'd come into the diner during high school or when his tour dates brought him back to Austin, the men had barely said two words to him.

It made her heart feel a little lighter knowing the people who mattered to her accepted Keaton. If she had any question about that, it was answered when they walked out from the kitchen to a round of cheers from the regular Monday night crowd.

Her first instinct was to pretend like everyone was making too big a deal of the situation, but Keaton took her hand and led her to a private booth in the corner.

"Why do I feel like I've aced my own sort of test tonight?"

She held her fingers over her mouth to stifle a giggle. "That might be true." She set her laptop next to her on the vinyl covered bench seat.

Ciara arrived at their table with a serving tray full of food and drink. She placed the roast chicken special in front of Keaton and gave Francesca her usual turkey Reuben sandwich with a side salad. They each had iced tea to drink and spent the meal talking and laughing.

"Am I crazy to say this is just as enjoyable as our night out on Saturday?" Keaton asked as he forked up a final bite of mashed potatoes.

Francesca pointed her fork at him. "You're just saying that because Lola May has promised you pie."

"It's because of you," he answered, his already piercing blue eyes turning so intense she struggled to catch her breath. "You make everything perfect."

"I'm glad you think so." She was more than glad. Her heart absolutely raced and tiny sparks danced up and down her spine. Just like her mother guessed, she was falling for Keaton. So hard and fast she wasn't sure if there was anything she could do to stop it. The truth was she didn't want to stop it. Somehow with

Keaton she felt a unique mix of nerves and comfort, as if he was exactly the right fit for her.

"But we still need pie," she told him when he continued to stare at her. "I'll grab us a slice to share." She stared to move out of the booth, butterflies dancing in her stomach.

Her knee knocked into the laptop, sending it flying off the seat. Francesca reacted as quickly as she could, horror slicing through her. She watched—in what seemed like slow motion—as the laptop crashed to the floor with a resounding crunch.

"No!" She went to her knees on the linoleum next to the thin computer. The screen had completely separated from the keyboard base. The corner of the computer that hit the floor first was dented. "My life is on there," she whispered, trying hard not to cry as she picked up both pieces. She'd saved for almost a year to buy that laptop and used it for every one of her classes.

Ciara, who was serving the booth behind them, turned to gaze down at Francesca. "Oh, honey, I'm sorry. Maybe it can be put back together."

"Maybe," she agreed, although she thought it would be easier to fix Humpty Dumpty than her broken laptop.

"A tech guru might be able to salvage the hard drive." Keaton had crouched down next to her and helped her to her feet.

"Do you think so?"

"Perhaps." He took the laptop from her and examined both sides. "I happen to have some inside connections at Robinson Tech. I'll call Wes and ask him to help or put me in touch with one of their gurus. We'll find someone to fix this."

It was difficult for Francesca to form a coherent thought. So far, her nerves around Keaton had made her drop a plate of hot food into his lap, almost spill a glass of wine on him and now she'd destroyed the computer she needed like it was an extra limb. "I appreciate the offer," she said slowly. "But I can't ask you to do that."

Keaton took her hand and gently squeezed her fingers. "You didn't ask. I offered." He tipped up her chin with his other hand. "Let me do this for you, Francesca. Please."

"Okay," she whispered. She forced air in and out of her lungs and sat back down in the booth. "Thank you. Let me know what you find out."

"Of course."

Lola May stopped by the table at that moment and set down two pieces of pie. "Dinner's on the house tonight," she said and gave Francesca's shoulders a squeeze. "Sorry about your computer, hon. The desktop in my office is ancient, but you're welcome to it anytime."

"Thanks, Lola May." Emotion clogged Francesca's throat at the thought of how many people she had in her life willing to help her. For so long, she'd been the one doing all the caregiving. She hadn't realized how tired it made her until she'd left Lou and his bandmates behind. Even as a girl, she'd had to make sure her mom took care of things. Paige would often forget to pay the rent or utilities—assuming she had the money—unless Francesca reminded her.

It sometimes felt like she'd been an adult for her entire life. As much as she didn't want to let herself rely on Keaton, having someone to share both the good and challenging details of her life was a pleasure. One she could come to depend on far too quickly.

Francesca was halfway through her shift the following day when Lola May waved her over. She finished taking the order from a family with three small kids then hurried to the far side of the counter where Lola May stood.

"It's like we're giving away food for free today," she said as she tucked a pencil behind her ear. "I haven't stopped running since I walked in this morning."

"I like the sound of that." The older woman glanced over Francesca's shoulder at the crowded restaurant. "I did what you told me and updated the diner's profile on some of the social networking sites and had the regulars do reviews for us. I think it's working."

Francesca blinked. "You took my advice?"

"Don't look so surprised," Lola May answered. "I know you're paying out the nose for those college classes. I also know you're learning a lot. You have great ideas when it comes to marketing. I'm not much for the internet, but even an old dog like me can learn a few new tricks."

"I'm glad my suggestions helped," Francesca said, pride bubbling up inside her.

"A messenger just dropped this off for you." Lola May tapped one pink-tipped fingernail on the wrapped package sitting on the edge of the counter.

"My birthday isn't for a couple of months." Francesca said, trailing a hand over the box. "What is it?"

"Why don't you open it so we can both find out," Lola May suggested.

"Right." The pink-papered box was tied with a wide

grosgrain ribbon in a darker shade of pink. Francesca tugged on it gently, then unwrapped the paper to reveal a white cardboard box with the image of a laptop and the Robinson Tech logo printed on it. There was a note taped to the top and her eyes widened as she scanned it.

"Well?" Lola May prompted.

"One of Keaton's brothers was able to retrieve the hard drive from my laptop, but the computer itself was ruined. He transferred all of my files to this laptop." Her gaze met Lola May's. "Keaton bought me a new computer."

The older woman chuckled softly. "Not exactly a diamond bracelet," she murmured, "but for you this is probably even better."

"I can't accept a gift like this," Francesca whispered, even as her heart raced with excitement. "It's too much."

"The boy wanted to get you a present." Lola May gathered up the wrapping paper and ribbon. "Let him spoil you a little, honey. You deserve it."

"You've got a five top that just came in." Brandi, the other waitress working today, hurried around the corner.

Francesca quickly nabbed the ribbon from Lola May and wound it around the laptop box. "Can you keep this in your office for me until I get a break?"

"Sure thing, Frannie."

Francesca put in the order for the family with the small children then went to greet the group that had just seated themselves in her section. She moved through the next two hours on autopilot, taking care of her section while joking with regular customers and even having a mini competition with Brandi to see who could encourage more diners to tag selfies taken at the diner on social media.

All the while, a strange sense of joy buzzed around inside her. Her body felt like it was filled with a thousand swirling bumblebees. The energy had her moving quickly, and she tried not to get distracted by thoughts of Keaton and the extravagant gift he'd sent her. She would, of course, offer to pay him. Still, the gesture meant so much to her because it showed that he understood what was important to her. He valued what she valued. The only gifts Lou had ever given her were cheap trinkets he'd bought from the counter at the convenience stores where he stopped for cigarettes. After walking away from him, Francesca had thrown away an assortment of magnets, shot glasses and fuzzy pens.

Without realizing it, Keaton had an uncanny ability to shine a light on some of the ways she'd let herself be undervalued in her previous relationship. No matter what her future held, Francesca vowed that she'd never allow a man to diminish her sense of self again.

By midafternoon, the restaurant was finally less crowded. She asked Brandi to cover her section while she took a break. Grabbing the laptop box from the cabinet in Lola May's office, she walked out the back of the diner then through the alley and across the street to the Austin Commons development site. She was heading toward the modular office when she spotted Keaton among a group of men in suits near the construction zone.

As if he sensed her presence, he lifted his gaze to hers and waved. A moment later he excused himself from the group and walked toward her. He wore a dark gray button-down shirt, tan pants and boots. Something about the combination gave him a more casual look than she was used to seeing, and she wondered if he was acclimating to life in Texas more than he even knew.

She certainly hoped that was the case. From what he'd told her, the first phase of Austin Commons was scheduled to open in June, and he planned to return to London after that. Her heart squeezed at the thought of Keaton living an ocean away.

"What a beautiful surprise," he said as he approached. He took off the yellow construction hat he wore and tucked it under one arm then bent to give her a gentle kiss.

"Someone might see," she whispered even as she lifted a finger to brush a lock of hair away from his face.

"I don't care," he said against her lips. He pulled back suddenly. "Do you?"

"Not at all."

He grinned like he was satisfied by her answer. "Aren't you working today?"

"I'm on break. I wanted to thank you for this." She held up the laptop box. "You didn't have to replace my computer."

"I wanted to." He shrugged like he was embarrassed she'd mentioned it. "It's not a big deal."

"Yes," she countered. "It is."

"You need a laptop for school."

"I do. But I can pay you back for the cost of this one." She gave a small laugh. "It might have to be in installments, but I'm willing to pay interest and—"

"Francesca, stop." He placed his big hands on her shoulders, and she loved the warmth that seeped through her T-shirt at his touch.

"I'm babbling," she muttered.

"The laptop is a gift," he said, his gorgeous eyes gentle. "A gift is something you don't pay for in any way. It's freely given."

"It's too much," she argued.

"No." A breeze kicked up, blowing a strand of hair into her face. He tucked it behind her ear. "I want to spoil you. If a computer is how I choose to do it, you're going to have to let me."

"Aren't you bossy?"

One side of his mouth kicked up. "Sometimes," he admitted. "And aren't you stubborn?"

"I suppose." She stuck out her tongue and he laughed. "Thank you, Keaton."

"You're welcome, Francesca."

Once again, the way he said her name made her knees go weak. "I should get back to the restaurant."

"Do you have plans after work?"

She smiled. "I think I'll be getting to know my new computer."

"I've put out most of the fires around here," he told her. "I was thinking of viewing a new photography exhibit at the Blanton Museum of Art. Would you accompany me?"

She loved the way he sometimes sounded so formal even as he was speaking so casually. "I'd like that."

"What time is your shift over?"

"Three."

"I'll pick you up then. We can have dinner at my apartment after."

She gave him a quick kiss then hurried back to the restaurant.

Ciara had just come in for her shift and greeted Francesca at the door. "A computer?" her friend asked when she had explained about her gift.

Francesca nodded.

"Not exactly a hopeless romantic, is he?"

"It was a sweet thought," Francesca answered, unwilling to share how much the gesture meant to her.

"I assume this means you're going to see him again?"

"After work. We're going to the Blanton Museum then to his place for dinner." Francesca scooted past Ciara. "I've got to put the laptop in Lola May's office and get back to work."

Ciara caught up with her in the hallway and grabbed her arm. "You know what this means, right?"

Francesca turned. "I don't have to grocery shop after my shift?"

"It's the *third* date," Ciara practically screeched.

"Who's got a third date?" Brandi asked, coming out of the women's restroom.

"Francesca and Keaton," Ciara said.

"The sexy British guy?" Brandi nodded. "Nice work for the girl we used to know as Frizzy Frannie. I didn't think you had it in you to nab a Fortune."

"I haven't nabbed anyone," Francesca said through clenched teeth. In the tight quarters in the hallway she hugged the laptop box close to her chest. She'd known Brandi since high school and hated that the other women mentioned her old nickname. All she wanted was to safely stow the computer in the office and return to work. She started toward the end of the hall.

"Better pull out the matching lingerie," Brandi called after her.

Francesca stopped, sucking a breath as she slowly turned back to face the other two waitresses. "Why do you say that?"

"You know what three dates mean, right?" Ciara asked.

"That we've gone out two other times?"

Ciara and Brandi both giggled like she was a silly toddler playing games. Although she'd been with Lou for over five years, sometimes Francesca felt like she knew next to nothing about how women and men were supposed to act while dating.

"It means there are expectations," Ciara explained. "Keaton will have expectations."

"Hopefully ones that involve cute undies," Brandi added, doing a little pelvic thrust. "It means it's time to get busy."

Francesca felt her eyes widen and quickly tried to feign indifference. "Things haven't gotten that serious with us," she said casually.

"It doesn't have to *be* serious to get down to serious business," Brandi said with a laugh. "Get with the times, girl. If you want to hook a guy like Keaton, you need to pony up. I'm sure his other women know what the third date means."

Francesca swallowed and darted a glance at Ciara. Her friend took the cue and put a hand on Brandi's arm. "We'd better get back out front before Lola May has a hissy fit. Francesca's got this covered. Right, Frannie?"

"You bet," Francesca answered. "I did laundry yesterday, so my matching lingerie is fluffed and folded."

Brandi rolled her eyes but followed Ciara down the hall. Francesca hurried through the kitchen and into the office, slamming the door shut behind her. She placed the laptop box on top of the file cabinet then fisted her hands at her sides, concentrating on pulling air in and out of her lungs.

Third date. Expectations. Cute undies.

She wasn't even sure if she owned cute undies anymore. For at least a year before they broke up, Lou hadn't seemed to have any interest in her sexually. He'd blamed it on being tired from his gigs, and she'd been naive enough to believe him. It wasn't until she found him in bed with a random groupie that she realized he'd had plenty of energy—just no interest in her.

She knew Keaton wanted her. Heck, he'd told her as much. But that only made her nerves spiral further out of control. He was handsome, charming and she knew he'd had plenty of girlfriends back in London. Did she even know how to live up to whatever expectations he had?

Or was the third date going to be her last with Keaton Fortune Whitfield?

Chapter Ten

As soon as Francesca got in the car, Keaton knew something was wrong. She looked beautiful in a casual wrap dress with a pattern of delicate flowers sewn into the fabric and a pair of faded red cowboy boots. The few inches of skin between the hem of the dress and the top of her boots made his body grow heavy with desire. At this point Francesca could wear a potato sack and it would turn him on.

But he couldn't miss the slight stiffening of her shoulders when he leaned in to kiss her. There was no mistaking the brittle edge to her voice, either, or the way her smile faltered when she thought he wasn't paying attention.

"How are things at the diner?" he asked as he steered the car through downtown Austin toward the U of T campus where the art museum was located.

"Fine."

"Busy shift?"

"Yep."

"Any interesting customers?"

"Nope."

Her hands were clasped tight in her lap. He reached over the console and pulled one into his, lacing their fingers together. "Is everything okay?"

She bit down on her lower lip before turning to him with a too-bright smile. "Just fine. I haven't been to the Blanton since a field trip in fifth grade."

Was his choice of an activity the problem? Keaton had to admit he'd never before taken a woman to a museum, other than for a gala opening of some sort. But he had a passion for black-and-white photography that he didn't share with many people. Normally his girlfriends only saw the side of him he wanted them to see—the charming bloke-about-town, the well-respected architect, the man who enjoyed good food and expensive wine. He wanted Francesca to know who he was underneath his mask, and it seemed like the photography exhibit would be a good place to start. Maybe he'd miscalculated. Or perhaps she was still not sure how to take his gift of the laptop?

He wanted to spoil Francesca. He wanted to give her all the things she'd never had in life. A little something niggled at the back of his mind, warning him that the one thing a woman like Francesca would want was the one thing he was unable to give—his heart.

But that was a worry for another time.

The museum's entrance was ahead, and he parked on the street a half a block away. The classical architecture and massive colonnades outside the three-story

building appealed to him and were a perfect comple-
ment to the campus buildings surrounding it.

He turned to face her and tightly held her hand
when she would have opened the door to exit. "What's
the problem, Francesca?"

"Wh-what do you mean?" she stammered, not
meeting his gaze. "I'm fine. We're fine. Let's go see
some photographs."

The last sentence was said with such fake enthusi-
asm it almost made his teeth ache.

"Something has changed since this afternoon," he
said softly. "What is it?"

She worried her lower lip for several moments before glancing up at him through her lashes. Her eyes
were so damned beautiful, big and brown. Yet the
worry he saw there was like a punch to the gut.

"This is our third date," she said finally, as if that
explained everything.

"I hope not our last."

Her brows furrowed. "I want there to be more
but…" She looked down to where their fingers were
linked, and smoothed her thumb back and forth along
the top of his hand. The touch was soft, like the but-
terfly kisses his mother used to flutter against his
cheeks with her eyelashes. "I'm a little worried about
meeting your *expectations*."

"My expectations?" he repeated.

She nodded. "A lot worried, actually." She kept
her gaze on their hands, now tracing figure-eight de-
signs on his skin.

"Francesca, would you look at me?"

Her lips pressed into a thin line, but she raised her
chin and met his gaze.

"What the hell are you talking about?" he asked her.

Her laughter rang through the interior of the car as her shoulders shook and she squeezed shut her eyes. "Third date sex," she said through another fit of giggles.

"Sex?" She might as well have knocked him on his arse with a cricket bat. He felt absolutely poleaxed by both her explanation and the fact that she couldn't stop laughing at the idea of having sex with him.

"You're experienced. I'm not." She made a face then dissolved into laughter again. "I'm messing up so bad, Keaton. This is who I am." She tugged her hand away from his and covered her face. "I babble when I'm nervous. I laugh at inappropriate times." She spread her fingers apart and stared at him through them. "What if I start laughing during sex?"

He inclined his head. "That would be a first for me."

"Right? Because you have expectations. *Expectations*." She drew out the syllables as if trying to teach a new word to a baby. "I've been with one man in my life. I probably don't even know…stuff." She gestured to him. "The kind of stuff you like and…"

"Expect?"

"Exactly."

"I *like* you," he told her. "I expect you to be honest and comfortable with whatever happens between us." He turned to face the front of the car and wrapped his hands around the steering wheel. "Until this moment, I've never regretted any of the women I've been with or how much experience I have." He slanted her a look. "Do I give off some sort of odd playboy vibe to you?"

She laughed again, only this time it sounded less

hysterical and more amused. At least that was a step in the right direction. "No. Of course not. It's me, not you."

"That might be the oldest brush-off line in the book."

"I'm not brushing you off," she argued. "But I don't want to disappoint you."

"If kissing you is any indication, nothing could be further from the truth."

"I shouldn't have said anything," she murmured. "But you wanted to know what was wrong, and that was it."

Keaton's world was filled with beautiful things—a stylish apartment, gorgeous women on his arm whenever he wanted, a career that afforded him every luxury. He'd worked hard for his success but had managed to move through his life without becoming emotionally invested in anyone.

Because of how he'd seen his mother suffer from a broken heart that wouldn't heal, he wasn't willing to risk his own. Discovering he was a Fortune had rocked his world in many ways, but he'd chosen to channel his energy into his search for Gerald's other illegitimate children. It was a way to be involved but still remain somewhat emotionally distant. His focus was on the task, not his feelings about all of the changes upending his own life and identity.

Without even realizing it, Francesca challenged him to open himself up in ways he never expected. She was pure emotion, always leading with her heart and true to how she felt at the moment. Even if how she felt made both of them crazy.

He blew out a breath, released the steering wheel

and turned to her again. "I'm glad you told me," he said. "But I don't give a damn about this theory of third-date expectations. I want to be with you, Francesca, because of who you are. Third date, fifth date, thirty-fourth date. Let's take this at our own pace. You and me."

The grin she gave him lit up her whole face and made everything else worth it. "So we can just concentrate on having fun?"

"I hope so," he said with a laugh. Although he couldn't imagine anything that would be more fun than taking this woman to his bed.

They entered the museum hand-in-hand, and a familiar happiness swept through Keaton. He'd forgotten how much he enjoyed meandering through the hushed galleries of an art museum, allowing the subtle lighting to guide his eye to various paintings, photographs and sculptures. With Francesca at his side, he found a whole new level of enjoyment.

They lingered at the photography exhibit he'd wanted to view but also visited several of the Blanton's permanent collections. Francesca told him stories about her elementary-school field trip and a boy from her class who had accidentally set off the building's fire alarm during the tour. He shared with her descriptions of his favorite London museums, particularly the British Museum, which had always been free to visit. The mix of antiquities and art from cultures around the world had fascinated him as a boy. While Austin was quickly coming to feel like home, Keaton had a sudden urge to share with Francesca all of his favorite spots in London.

They stayed at the museum until it closed, then

Keaton ordered carryout from a Thai restaurant one of his coworkers recommended. He and Francesca sat on the floor of his apartment in front of the coffee table as they ate, watching the original James Bond movie starring Sean Connery.

"I could see you as James Bond," she told him, taking a bite of Pad Thai. "You have the right accent."

"Half of England has the right accent," he said. "I think I'd do okay with the fast cars but I'll leave the guns to 007."

"You're definitely handsome enough."

"Thank you." He nudged her with his elbow. "Would you be my Bond girl?"

She snorted. "I'd make a horrible Bond girl. Can you imagine me as Ursula Andress coming out of the ocean in my white bikini?"

"Yes, I can." He dropped a kiss on her shoulder. "Quite clearly in fact."

Francesca was careful only to drink one glass of wine with dinner. Her body was already on high alert just from being so near Keaton. It was difficult to believe a museum date was the most romantic thing she'd ever experienced, but somehow it was still true.

Once she'd told Keaton about her third-date fears, the knot of panic that had been holding her heart captive loosened and eventually dissolved into nothing. Saying the words out loud had removed the power they had over her. She believed Keaton when he told her he didn't expect anything from her she wasn't comfortable giving. It felt amazing to be with a man who truly cared about her feelings and didn't just see her as a reflection of himself.

The Thai food was fabulous and the conversation flirty and easy as they watched James Bond save the world from the evil Dr. No. When the movie ended, she stood and began to clear the plates and carryout containers but Keaton gently pushed her to the sofa.

"You're on your feet all day," he told her. "Let me take care of you for a bit."

As she watched him gather everything and take it to the kitchen, she had to admit that a man cleaning up was ridiculously sexy. In reality, everything Keaton did was sexy to her.

He returned a few minutes later and sat next to her then pulled her legs into his lap and took one of her bare feet in his hands. She'd taken off her boots and socks when they'd arrived at his apartment, preferring as always to be barefoot whenever she had the chance. Tonight, though, she wondered if it had been in unconscious preparation for Keaton.

He began to gently massage her foot, kneading the sensitive arch with his strong hands.

"That is amazing," she whispered, letting her head fall back against the couch cushions. "I bet not even James Bond has such talented hands."

Keaton only chuckled and switched his attention to her other foot. A moment later, she let out a soft moan as he hit a particularly sensitive spot.

"I like the polish," he said and she forced open her eyes to glance down at her feet.

"My mom used to do nails," she explained, wiggling her toes. "Ever since I was little, our Sunday ritual has been for her to paint my toenails. She likes to experiment on me with her nail art."

Right now Francesca's toes were colored a soft pink

hue with little flowers painted on her big toes. A tiny purple gem sparkled at the tip of each flower petal.

"Your toes are a work of art," he said and then slid his hands up her calves before tugging her closer. "Actually, that could be said for your entire body."

She opened her mouth to argue, because that's what women like her did when receiving a compliment from a handsome, sexy, charming man. She might have left Fat Frannie behind years ago, but Francesca still saw herself as that pudgy, insecure girl with the ill-fitting clothes and flyaway hair.

Male customers at Lola May's sometimes flirted with her, but Keaton's attention felt different. Real. Intense.

As difficult as it was for her to imagine he meant the words, if he wanted to tell her she was beautiful...well, Francesca would just have to suck it up and accept the praise. The silliness of her internal struggle made her giggle, and a slow grin spread across Keaton's face as he pulled her into his lap.

"Nervous?" he asked, nuzzling the underside of her jaw with his nose.

"No," she whispered on a sigh. "We're having fun."

"The *most* fun," he agreed and claimed her mouth.

The kiss started as a gentle tease, like he was giving her time to acclimate to him. But even without alcohol buzzing through her system, desire flamed in her like a brushfire, burning away all her nerves until she was left with nothing but her need for him.

As if he could read her mind—or at least her body—Keaton deepened the kiss. His tongue swept into her mouth at the same time his palm grazed up the bare skin of her leg and just under the hem of her dress.

She welcomed the touch, wanted everything this man could give her. She wound her hands around his neck, pressing closer to him. His body was hot and hard against her and she lost herself in the feel of him.

His fingers inched up her thigh and curled into the fabric of her panties. The sensation overwhelmed her, forcing her to pull back as she tried to catch her breath.

"I don't have matching lingerie," she told him. "Just so you know."

"I don't give a damn." He kissed her again, and the words he spoke tickled her lips. "Just so you know."

After that, Francesca stopped talking other than to give whispered demands. *Yes. There. More. Now.*

He really didn't need any direction from her. Keaton knew exactly how she liked to be touched, and every stroke of his fingers drove her closer to the edge. But he listened and incorporated her breathy commands into the blinding pleasure he was giving her. As his fingers worked against her, he continued to kiss her and it wasn't long before a brilliant pressure built inside her.

"Open for me," he murmured and she did without hesitation, too consumed by desire to be concerned with nerves or doubts. She gave herself over to the moment, and it was better than she could have imagined. When she would have rushed her release, he slowed his movements like he had all night to devote himself to her pleasure.

Eventually she couldn't hold on any longer. The pressure and need coalesced to a fever pitch. With a cry that Keaton caught in his mouth, she broke apart.

It felt like a thousand shooting stars rained down on her, the light behind her eyes a shower of sparkles.

She held on to him as she came back to reality, realizing as she opened her eyes that he'd straightened her dress and now traced lazy circles on her back with the same hand that had sent her over the edge just minutes before. That had been the most amazing experience of her life, and she hadn't even taken off her clothes. What would it be like to have sex with this man? The thought boggled her mind.

He pressed a kiss to the top her head. "See how much fun we can have without expectations?"

"I had tons of fun. A million sparkles worth of fun."

He chuckled. "A million sparkles are good for my ego."

"What about *your* fun?" she asked.

He pulled away just enough to look into her eyes. The tenderness she saw there took her breath away. "Giving you pleasure is the best sort of fun for me. I plan to have many, many more opportunities to show you just how much fun we can have together."

"I can't wait," she whispered.

Chapter Eleven

"Need coffee now." Francesca stumbled out of her bedroom toward the small kitchen the next morning. It was almost seven, and she wanted to shower before her morning class. She wasn't scheduled to work at Lola May's, which was the only bright spot looming in her day.

Before she'd even made it to the counter, Ciara thrust a steaming mug into her hand.

"I didn't hear you come in last night," Ciara said with a slight smirk. "Must have been a late one."

"I fell asleep watching a movie at Keaton's," Francesca mumbled.

Ciara winked. "Which is code for…"

"For I fell asleep," Francesca snapped, "and didn't get back here until after midnight." That part didn't bother her. It had been lovely to drift to sleep snuggled against Keaton's chest. But after he'd walked her to her door, given her a slow kiss and said good-night, Francesca hadn't been able to fall asleep again.

She should have been relaxed after her night with him, but she'd tossed and turned for hours. Her body, which had been so sated earlier in the evening, had continued to hum with need.

More. She wanted more. And she could have had it if she hadn't let her stupid third-date insecurities engulf her.

Ciara took a sip of coffee. "Where's your glow?"

Francesca opened the fridge and pulled out her favorite vanilla creamer, dumping double her normal allotment into the coffee. "What glow?"

"Your post-sex glow. You can't expect me to believe a man like Keaton can't give you a glow. Heck, just looking at him makes me—"

"I don't," Francesca ground out, slamming shut the fridge door, "want to know what he makes you feel." She gulped down half the coffee then reached for the pot to refill her mug. "I'm glowing."

"You're growling."

"I didn't sleep well."

"I hope because he kept you awake all night?"

Francesca set both the coffee pot and her mug on the counter with a thump. "We didn't have sex," she shouted.

Ciara blinked. "Okay."

Tears rushed to Francesca's eyes. "It's not okay. It's the opposite of okay."

"Did you and Keaton have a fight?" Ciara's voice was gentle.

"Nothing like that. It was a great date. The best.

And we...he...stuff happened. Fun stuff." She blew out a breath, remembering the feel of Keaton's hands on her. "Amazing stuff. But not sex." She glanced up at her long-time friend. "It's your fault."

Ciara took a step back. "What did I do?"

"You mentioned third-date expectations," Francesca answered miserably. "I freaked out. Keaton was totally understanding, but it slowed things down." She picked up her coffee and took another huge swallow. "Maybe it's better. I don't even own cute undies anymore. Why would I have needed them with Lou? He didn't want to have sex with me. But Keaton does— or at least he did. And I—"

"Need to go easy on the caffeine," Ciara said, nabbing the mug out of her hand. "I'm sorry, Frannie. I didn't mean to send you into a panic. You deserved some third-date fun. But you know it doesn't matter when it happens. There's no official timeline."

"I want it to happen," Francesca said, running a hand through her tangle of curls. "Now I feel like every time we go on a date, what didn't happen last night will be hanging over us."

Ciara snickered. "I hope you don't mean literally."

"Get your mind out of the gutter," Francesca said, but it felt good to laugh with her friend. "What am I going to do?"

"What time are you done with class this morning?"

"Nine thirty."

Ciara looked up at the clock that hung above the kitchen sink. "Perfect. The mall opens at ten. The first thing you're going to do is buy some lingerie. Lots of lingerie."

"I don't need lots," Francesca protested.

"You do. Next, you're going to take matters into your own hands." She pointed a finger at Ciara. "Not literally but we're not ruling that out as an option."

Francesca grabbed the mug from the counter. "I definitely need more coffee to decipher what you're trying to tell me."

"I'm talking about a booty call."

Francesca paused with the mug halfway to her mouth. "Excuse me?"

"You're worried about getting nervous on a date with Keaton, right?"

"Right."

"You need to take the thing that's making you nervous off the table." She giggled. "So to speak."

"Enough with the innuendos," Francesca said.

"Invite him over for sex."

Ciara said the words calmly, like she was suggesting Francesca and Keaton take high tea together.

"I can't...do...that." Francesca's heart raced even thinking about it.

"Yes, you can." Ciara rubbed her palms together like she was some sort of diabolical seduction mastermind. "It's the perfect solution."

"What if he says no?"

Ciara flipped her long hair over one shoulder. "He's not going to say no. Stop thinking every man is like Lou the Louse. You've spent too long selling yourself short, Frannie. When you left Lou it was to make a new life for yourself."

"And I have," Francesca said, but she knew it wasn't quite true. She'd come back to the same job she'd had since she was sixteen, and while college was a big step for her, she used the restaurant and her studies as an excuse to put her personal life on the back burner. Yes, she was busy. But as the past two weeks with Keaton had proved, she could make time for the right man.

The right man.

That was the key. Although she was reluctant to label it, whatever was between her and Keaton felt right. It was time to take a step toward claiming the life she wanted.

If she needed cute undies to make it happen, then so be it.

"I'll meet you at the mall at ten," she told Ciara before wrapping her friend in a tight hug.

Ciara gave a little squeal of delight. "Operation British Seduction is a go?"

Francesca grinned. "It's a go."

"What did that cow do to make you so mad?"

Keaton stared across the table at Ben Robinson. "What are you talking about?"

Ben's thick brow lifted. "You're cutting into that piece of meat like you have a personal vendetta against it."

Keaton glanced down at the steak he'd ordered and realized he was, indeed, sawing at it with the knife like he was Jack the Ripper. He carefully placed his utensils on the edge of the plate. "It's nothing. I've got a lot on my mind."

That statement was both true and false. He had only one thing in his mind—a deliciously curvy waitress with blond hair tumbling down her back. Thoughts of Francesca consumed him until there seemed to be no room left in his brain for anything else.

"We'll track down the other Fortunes," Ben told

him, misinterpreting what was agitating Keaton. The assumption was better than his half brother guessing the true reason. One thing Keaton had learned in his short time having brothers and sisters—siblings were a nosy lot.

After his visit with Graham, Keaton had fielded a phone call from Olivia and a stream of texts from the youngest Robinson, Sophie. Both women had been far too curious about the state of his personal life and the hints Graham had dropped about Keaton's love life. He'd managed to answer their questions in a way that seemed to satisfy them without giving away anything about his relationship with Francesca. He'd learned a few lessons being raised by his mother and her posse of prying friends.

"I have a better lead on the French Fortune," Keaton said. "The time difference makes it a bit of a challenge to speak in real time, but my friend who lives in Paris reports that Amersen Beaudin might be the man we want."

"This is Suzette's son?" Ben asked, his voice tight.

"Yes. I want to be completely certain before we approach him, especially given your family's history with his mother." It was a sticking point with all the Robinson children that their father left so many broken hearts, as well as fatherless children, in his wake. He thought the fact that their former au pair was the mother of one of them might be particularly difficult to accept.

Ben nodded then said, "I've located Chloe Elliott living right here in Austin. She works as a counselor. It sounds crazy, but she grew up just down the road from us. I don't think I ever knew her, but it certainly hits close to home."

"Text me her information," Keaton told Ben. "I can get in touch with her."

"What about Nash Tremont? Any leads on the Oklahoma Fortune?" Ben took a bite of his club sandwich. They'd met for lunch downtown, and Keaton had once again been tempted to invite Ben to Lola May's. But something stopped him. Last night with Francesca had been amazing, but he wanted to make sure she felt the same way he did before he introduced her to his family.

He was certain his Fortune siblings would approve of her, which might be the reason behind his hesitation. His feelings for Francesca were a jumble, and he wasn't sure he could handle the pressure of having his brothers and sisters push him to take things to the next level.

"Tremont is dodging my calls and ignoring my texts." Keaton shrugged. "I don't want to push too hard or we could lose him. It's hard to know how each person will take the news or if they're even interested in knowing they have a new family."

"Most people are interested in becoming a Fortune. Speaking of which, did you meet with that reporter?"

"Ariana Lamonte." Keaton nodded. "She emailed me some initial questions and the actual interview is scheduled for tomorrow morning. The piece will run on *Weird Life*'s blog first, then an expanded interview will go in the print magazine."

"You've kept a low profile for a Fortune," Ben observed. "After this there'll be no more anonymity for you."

"I get that," Keaton answered. "But if one of Gerald's other illegitimate children reads the article and is helped by it, then the additional publicity will be worth it." He pointed his fork toward Ben. "Ariana definitely sees 'Becoming a Fortune' as a series. She may want to spotlight one or two of the Robinsons, as well."

Ben shook his head. "Not me right now. If she wants to talk to someone else, send her to Sophie or Olivia first. When this baby comes, I'm going to have my hands more than full."

"Will do. I'll let them decide who wants to be the next…"

"Victim?" Ben supplied with a wry grin.

"Newsmaker," Keaton countered.

Just then Keaton's phone began to buzz in his back pocket. He pulled it out to see Francesca's number flashing across the screen. Holding up a finger to let Ben know he'd only be a minute, he slid his thumb across the screen to answer.

"Hello, luv," he murmured, keeping his voice low enough that Ben wouldn't hear.

"Is this Keaton?" an unfamiliar voice asked.

His shoulders stiffened. "Yes. Who's this?"

"It's Ciara James, Francesca's roommate. We've met at the restaurant and—"

"Where's Francesca? Is she okay?" He knew he'd raised his voice when Ben lifted a brow, but at this point Keaton didn't care. An uncomfortable rush of panic shot through him at the thought that Francesca might be in trouble and unable to use the phone herself.

"She's fine," Ciara answered quickly. "But she needs you to come to our apartment. No emergency. No rush." There was a rustling on the other end of the line. "Maybe a little rush wouldn't hurt. Just get here when you can, okay?"

"Can I talk to her?"

It sounded like Ciara put her hand over the mouthpiece. There were muffled voices then she returned to the line. "I don't think so. She'll be here when you arrive."

"Why can't she—"

He stopped speaking when the line went dead.

"Damn." He stared at the screen, as if willing the phone to ring again. "I've got to go."

"Does this have anything to do with your waitress?"

"I wouldn't say she's mine," Keaton said, but his heart squeezed at the denial. He might not want to admit it, but she certainly felt like she belonged to him.

"You don't have to," Ben told him. "Graham filled us in."

"Siblings are a pain in the arse," Keaton muttered.

Ben threw back his head and laughed. "You've been a Fortune a full year now. Has it really taken you this long to realize that? I thought you Brits were quicker on the uptake." Ben made shooing motions with his hands, much like Keaton's mother had done when he was boy bothering her in the kitchen as she worked to put supper on the table. "You'd better go. I've seen the signs. You've got it bad."

"No, it was just a strange phone call," Keaton argued. "Francesca and I are just having fun. It isn't serious." But his body was seriously screaming for him to bolt out of the restaurant and rush to her side as quickly as he could.

"You sound like me this time last year. We'll see

what happens next. I'm guessing there will be wedding bells in your future before you know it. But right now go. Hell, you're making me nervous with the time you're wasting."

Keaton stood from the table. "You're wrong about the wedding bells, but thanks for understanding about cutting short our lunch."

"Text later and let me know how things worked out."

With a nod, Keaton turned, striding out of the restaurant and into the bright noonday Texas sun. He'd parked around the block and jogged to his car. It was a quick ten minute drive through town to the SoCo neighborhood and Lola May's. Ciara was waiting for him at the bottom of the stairs that led up to the apartment she and Francesca shared.

"She's up there," the leggy brunette told him. "I'll be gone for a while." She leaned in closer. "A *long* while."

He didn't press her for an explanation. Instead, Keaton took the stairs two at a time, his heart pounding like he'd just swum the English Channel. The door to the apartment was slightly ajar and he pushed through, searching for Francesca in the strangely dim light.

"Thanks for coming over so quickly."

She stood in the middle of the room, between the kitchen and the sofa, her fingers drumming on the back of a chair.

"Is everything okay?" He took a step toward her, his eyes scanning up and down to try to discern if she was hurt in some way. She looked fine. She looked...

Keaton stopped dead in his tracks when he realized Francesca wore only a thin, silk robe in a deep ruby color that made her skin glow as if illuminated from within. Then he noticed the votive candles that flickered from the top of every surface in the room.

"Everything is fine," she murmured. "Better than fine, I hope."

A shy smile curving her lips, she slowly undid the robe's sash.

Keaton's mouth went dry at the glimpse of red that peeked out from the gap in the fabric. A moment later, Francesca slipped the robe from her shoulders. It pooled in a puddle at her feet, leaving her in nothing but the sexiest damn bra and panty set he could have imagined in his wildest dreams.

A shiver raced through Keaton at the same time that all his brain cells hurtled south, leaving his mind completely blank.

Francesca licked her dry lips and waited for Keaton to say something. Anything.

He continued to stare at her without speaking for several long moments. She was suddenly terrified that she'd gotten it wrong. What if he wasn't interested in being seduced by her?

Heart stammering, she bent and grabbed for the robe.

"Don't."

The word hung in the air, almost echoing in the charged quiet of the apartment. She straightened but couldn't help covering her midsection and chest with her hands.

Keaton still stood only a foot or so inside her door, his arms stiffly at his sides.

"Let me see you." His voice was a low rumble. "Please."

She dropped her arms. "No emergency," she said with a shaky laugh. She'd made the decision to close the blinds and light candles after her trip to the mall with Ciara. It was one thing to greet a man wearing little more than her birthday suit. It was another to do it in broad daylight.

Keaton didn't smile, and she couldn't read his expression.

"I'm sorry if I worried you," she said automatically. "I just wanted…" How could she explain all the things she wanted from Keaton when she barely understood them herself? In the end, she settled for murmuring, "You."

He closed the distance between them in three long strides but didn't reach for her. "You took about a decade off my life with that phone call."

"I'm so—"

He put a finger to her lips. "But it was worth every year for this moment. You are the most beautiful thing I've ever seen."

"I bought cute panties," she whispered.

His eyes never left her face. "The lingerie is fantastic, but it's you that makes it so amazing. Are you sure this is what you want? There are no expectations, no special time frame. I'm willing to wait as long as it takes. You're worth it, Francesca."

"I want this. I want you, Keaton. No more waiting."

As if he'd been longing to hear those words, he snaked an arm around her waist and pulled her tight against him. His other hand fisted in her hair, tugging

back her head so that her throat was exposed. He bent
his head and trailed hot kisses along her neck.

Heat radiated from him, and the fabric of his crisp
white shirt scraped against her lace bra, making her
breasts grow heavy with need.

As if he read her mind, his hand left her hair to cup
one breast, his thumb grazing over her nipple. She
moaned in response and he deepened the kiss even
further. When her knees gave way, he scooped her into
his arms. "Bedroom?" he whispered against her lips.

She pointed to the door past the kitchen, unable to
speak beyond a heated sigh.

He carried her in and kicked the door shut with his
heel. A moment later she felt her cool sheets against
her back and gave herself a mental gold star for having
the foresight to pull back the quilt earlier. She pushed
at his chest when he came down over top of her.

"You're wearing too many clothes."

"Indeed I am," he agreed.

When he stood, she reached for the quilt to pull
over her but Keaton shook his head. "Leave it," he
commanded, his voice a hoarse rasp. He started on
the buttons of his shirt, his finger trembling slightly
as he worked at them.

An unfamiliar feeling of power washed through
Francesca. This man was as affected by her as she
was by him. She drew up her knee and sat forward
slightly, knowing it would push up her breasts, and
was rewarded by a low growl from Keaton.

Maybe she was better at seduction than she'd
thought.

Then he reached the last button and slid the shirt off
his shoulders. He had the most delicious chest she'd

ever seen, with lean muscles and just the right amount of dark hair swirling around his nipples. Francesca's mouth went dry and all she could think was *yes*.

She was so intent on memorizing the hard planes of his upper body that she didn't even realize he'd stripped totally until she heard the rip of the condom packet. Once he'd sheathed himself, he climbed onto the bed again.

"This is the best way I can think of to spend an afternoon," Keaton whispered.

She automatically opened her thighs for him, and cupping her face between his palms, his gaze intent on hers, he moved into her in one long stroke.

Francesca gasped, both from the pleasure of it and the intimacy of the moment. She'd never imagined it could be like this. Keaton stilled, and she could feel the willpower it took for him not to move.

"Does it—"

Before he could finish the question, she wrapped a hand around his neck and fused his mouth to hers. At the same time she rocked her hips to take him deeper. He let out a soft groan and they began to move together. It was too much and not enough. All she wanted was to stay in his arms forever.

There was no place she ended and he began. They were simply one. Francesca lost herself in a torrent of movement, sensation and whispered words. How could she have ever doubted how perfect it would feel to be with Keaton? From the first, everything about him was different. With each thoughtful gesture and sweet flirtation, he'd crept past her defenses. Now there was no part of her that didn't belong to him—

her body, her heart. Everything that had come before now seemed like a placeholder for this moment.

The thought drove her even further into the sparkling swell of desire and she held him tighter. Minutes later her whole world burst and she arched up, unable to hold back her response. It felt like she was exploding from the inside out, a shower of light radiating through her body and making every inch of her flame into oblivion.

Keaton was there to catch each of her cries, moving until at last she felt him shudder around her. Slowly she came back to herself as Keaton flipped to his back and tucked her into him, fanning her curls across his chest.

"I have no words," he whispered, "for how unbelievable that was."

"Those are pretty good ones," she teased.

He dropped a gentle kiss on the top of her head. "You scared the bloody hell out of me with that phone call, but I'll race halfway across the world to get to your side for that."

She lifted her head so she could meet his gaze. She saw the hint of amusement there but also a deep tenderness that stole her breath for a moment. Could it be that he was falling for her in the same way she was for him?

Francesca was used to being the one to have to make a bigger effort, but she'd always craved more. After Lou, she'd promised herself not to settle for anything less than a man who loved her the way she wanted to be loved. Her heart gave a little leap at the thought that she might have found that with Keaton.

"Ciara was only supposed to ask you to come to

the apartment," she explained, "not to scare the pants off you."

He laughed and drew her closer for a long kiss. "Anytime you want my pants off, Francesca-luv," he said, "I'm more than happy to oblige."

Then he spent the rest of the afternoon demonstrating exactly how obliging he could be.

Chapter Twelve

As Keaton entered the restaurant where he was meeting Ariana Lamonte the next morning, his thoughts strayed to Francesca. Truth be told, there had scarcely been a moment since he'd left her apartment yesterday afternoon that she hadn't been in his mind.

He'd never experienced anything like the way the feisty waitress had invaded his senses. He caught faint traces of her vanilla scent on the air even when she wasn't with him and just thinking of the sweet sounds she'd made under him made his body harden.

His dinner with the developer of the Austin Commons project had gone late last night and he hadn't seen Francesca again. He'd already texted to make sure she was available after her shift at the diner today. There was no way he could go another night without holding her in his arms. She was like a drug. With one hit he'd become hopelessly addicted.

He scanned the restaurant for Ariana, but his gaze caught on a man rising from a table near the back.

Gerald Robinson.

Keaton's biological father turned, as if he could feel the weight of Keaton's stare. Clearly, Gerald had been perfecting his bland mask of civility for years— Keaton guessed being a serial adulterer would force a man to keep his emotions under strict control. Other than a slight widening of his cool blue eyes, Gerald didn't immediately react to Keaton's presence in the restaurant.

Keaton held his father's gaze, unsure of how to proceed. He certainly wasn't going to talk to the man. They'd had one strained conversation last year at Zoe's wedding to Joaquin Mendoza that Keaton wasn't anxious to repeat. As close as he was to his Robinson half siblings, Keaton's feelings toward Gerald weren't so straightforward.

Seeing Gerald in person, acknowledging his own connection to a man who seemed to leave behind a trail of unwanted children like a schoolboy discards empty candy wrappers, made Keaton's blood run cold. After another moment, Gerald inclined his head slightly, as if he'd taken Keaton's measure and now deigned to give his paternal approval.

That rankled, too, and Keaton turned away. He refused to take anything from his father—even a tacit acknowledgment. An image of Francesca flashed again in Keaton's mind, and his hands balled into fists at his sides. How had he ever believed he could be the type of man she deserved when Gerald Robinson's blood ran through his veins?

At Zoe's wedding, Gerald had said one sentence to Keaton that had stuck in his head, refusing to let go.

You remind me of myself as a younger man.

Some small, secret place in Keaton—the angry boy who'd had something to prove to the father he never knew—had preened at the comparison. But the man in him recoiled thinking he shared anything with Gerald.

"Sorry I'm late."

Keaton jerked as a hand came to rest on his arm. He glanced down to see Ariana offering him a tentative smile. She searched his face then asked, "Is everything okay?"

He drew in a deep breath. "Fine. Let's get started, shall we?"

She watched him for another moment and he offered what he hoped was a charming smile. "They've held a table for me in the corner," she said finally. "It will give us some privacy."

As they moved through the restaurant, a busboy turned abruptly, almost plowing into Ariana. Automatically, Keaton placed a hand on her back and guided her out of the way. He couldn't help a final glance toward Gerald, who was now watching with a knowing smile curving one side of his mouth. Keaton snatched his hand away from the reporter, hating that anyone might think he was cut from the same philandering cloth as his father. Even though he hadn't promised anything to Francesca, he couldn't imagine being interested in another woman.

He enjoyed talking to Ariana but could no more conjure a physical attraction to her than he might feel toward one of his half sisters. Still, the look from Gerald was seared into his brain and he barely registered the questions Ariana asked him.

When he walked out of the restaurant an hour later, he couldn't have repeated any of the answers he'd given during the interview. Ariana had seemed satisfied and told him the blog would run on Friday with a follow-up in the magazine's next issue.

Back at the office, there was the normal barrage of meetings, questions from the contractor and the junior architects assigned to the project.

It wasn't until hours later when he stepped into Lola May's and heard the familiar peal of Francesca's bubbly laugh that the tight knot of tension in his stomach loosened. Several of the regular customers he'd come to know over the past few weeks greeted him and the scent of freshly baked apple pie made his stomach rumble. In such a short time this place and these people had come to feel like they belonged to him. Like he was part of a community—different from the friends and coworkers he'd had in London. He didn't have to be anything but himself at Lola May's. When Francesca turned to him, the grin that lit up her face made him feel like the queen had just knighted him.

She moved toward him, as if the same invisible magnet that drew him also pulled her.

"You're early," she said. "Did you know we had warm pie?"

He shook his head, swallowing the emotion that balled in his throat. Her caramel-colored eyes were clear and tender, the color high on her cheeks as she approached him.

"I just wanted to see you." He reached for her, unable to stop himself from wrapping his arms around her, and seared his mouth to hers, fast and hard.

Francesca squeaked but she opened for him and he felt a shiver run through her. A few whistles and cat calls rang out through the diner, and Keaton released her with a smile. "Sorry," he said, although he wasn't sorry at all. He wanted to shout from the rooftops that this woman belonged to him.

She pressed her fingertips to her lips and gave him a little shake of her head. "I don't believe that for a second. You look far too smug."

"Maybe," he admitted. "I'll wait for you to finish your shift."

"Thank you for the flowers," she whispered. "They're beautiful."

He'd had a bouquet of yellow roses sent over this morning, although it had been difficult to order only one. He wanted to fill her entire apartment with blooms, but he understood now that he'd be better off not overwhelming her. He'd settled for placing a standing order to be delivered every week for the next three months. He might have to take it slow, but he was still determined to spoil Francesca until she realized she was worthy of getting everything she ever wanted from a man. And that he was the man to give it to her.

"Keaton, come and sit a spell at the counter," Lola May called. "Our girl has customers and I need someone to try the first bite of this salted caramel apple pie and make sure it tastes as good as it smells."

"I'm at your service," he answered then lowered his voice to a husky whisper. "Until later," he told Francesca, "when I'm at your service."

* * *

The perfect bubble of happiness that had started inside Francesca on the afternoon she spent in bed with Keaton grew over the next week until it felt like she was floating through her days in an effervescent pocket of joy and—

Not love. She wouldn't allow herself to consider the word *love*.

But the harder she tried not to think of it, the more she felt it. Till she finally had to admit it. She'd fallen in love with Keaton—the kind of love that made her heart feel like it would beat out of her chest every time she was with the handsome Brit.

Of course she hadn't told Keaton she loved him. She might have lost her heart, but thankfully her mind was still functioning. Keaton felt something for her. It was evident in every touch and look he gave her. But he'd made no promises or said anything other than beguiling words whispered late at night when he held her. She knew what could happen when she gave more than someone was willing to give back. She had no interest in repeating that sort of heartache again.

She tried to convince herself that what they had was enough. Keaton was attentive and sweet, thoughtful and funny. She'd never imagined she could be so attracted to a man and had spent every night of the past week at his apartment. He seemed to know what she wanted and how she liked to be touched even before she did. Every moment she spent in his arms was a gift, and she refused to entertain thoughts of her blissful bubble popping.

A knock on the apartment door interrupted her musings. She glanced at the clock on the wall. It was almost ten on a Saturday morning, and she didn't have to be downstairs for her shift until noon. She'd slipped out of Keaton's bed this morning, despite his protests, to return to her apartment and work on a paper that was due next week.

Ciara had left to run errands so Francesca hurried to the door, assuming her roommate had forgotten the apartment key again.

"You're back soon," she said as she opened the door.

"I knew you missed me," came the gravelly response.

Francesca's mouth went dry and she tried to slam closed the door but Louis Rather, aka Lou the Louse, walked into her apartment as if he owned the place. Lou's confidence had been one of the things that had first drawn Francesca to him. Now it was irritating and unwarranted.

She had to admit he still looked good. His dark blond hair was slicked back into an almost pompadour and he wore faded jeans and a tight black Henley under the well-worn leather jacket she'd given him their first Christmas on the road. Lou wasn't as tall or broad as Keaton, but he'd perfected the bad-boy indie rocker look. Taming the bad boy had once appealed to Francesca, but she no longer had time for jerks in her life.

Absently, she ran a hand over the old T-shirt and yoga pants she'd changed into for a morning of studying. It would have been nice to at least have taken a shower before a long-overdue and unwanted confrontation with her philandering ex-boyfriend.

"Don't bother making yourself at home, Lou," she

told him, even as he strode toward the kitchen. "You aren't staying."

"I need caffeine," he said over his shoulder. "And no one makes coffee as good as you, Frannie. Now be a good girl and point me in the direction of a mug."

When he turned, she crossed her arms over her chest and tapped her bare foot against the hardwood floor. "Get out."

He gave a belabored sigh and opened cabinet doors until he found the mugs. He poured a cup of coffee and took a long drink, hitching one hip onto the counter. "Damn, I've missed you," he whispered and Francesca honestly wasn't sure if he was talking to her or the coffee.

"Get out," she repeated.

"I need to talk to you," he said, his blue gaze ridiculously pleading and soft as he met her gaze. It had been those tiny moments of tenderness that had made her such a fool for him. Months before she'd caught him—pants down—with the groupie, Francesca had suspected Lou of cheating on her. Then he would meet her gaze while performing one of the band's rare ballads on stage, looking at her in a secret way that she assumed he saved only for her. Every time he'd sucked her back into trusting him.

Those days were over.

"What do you want?" she asked him.

He stared at her a moment, then his brows drew low, as if he couldn't understand why his usual charm wasn't working.

"I'm back in Austin until spring," he told her, setting the coffee cup on the counter. "Cowbell is recording some tracks at a local studio. We're working with a famous producer, Frannie, and the label is putting a ton of money into the new album. It's going to be big."

"I'm glad for you," she said, and found that despite what he'd done to her, she meant the words. Lou might be a unfaithful jackass, but he was a talented musician. "What does that have to do with me?"

He gave a boyish shrug. "I thought we could spend some time together. You know, like back in the good old days when it was just you and me."

"You and me and whatever fangirl you were messing around with while I was doing the band's laundry."

"My clothes haven't been that clean since you left," he told her with a placating smile.

She snorted. "Seriously? Is the opportunity to be your maid supposed to entice me back? You couldn't possibly have run out of groupies so quickly."

"I want *you*," he said firmly. "I miss *you*. Not as a maid." He straightened and took a step toward her. "I'll take you on dates this time around, Frannie. There are some new alt punk bands in town I want to check out. We can go to the shows together."

"I don't like alt punk music, Lou."

His head snapped back as if she'd punched him. She wasn't sure she'd ever given her true opinion on anything in all the years they were together. Shame on her for being a pushover. But no longer.

"What's happened to you, Francesca? You've changed."

"I've grown up," she countered. "I'm not that same people-pleasing girl who was grateful for whatever crumbs of attention you were willing to throw my way. I've realized I deserve more. Better. I deserve to be with a man who values me and wants to make me happy."

He took a step toward her. "You think you've found that?"

Although Francesca was reluctant to put a name on whatever she had with Keaton, there was no denying how he made her feel. "I'm in a relationship with a man," she said quietly. "He cares about me. I'm happy."

Lou stared at her a few long moments. "You do deserve happiness," he said finally. "I'm just sorry I couldn't be the guy to give it to you."

She started to offer words that would absolve him of the responsibility because that was her way, but Lou spoke first.

"But I hope you haven't pinned your hopes on catching that new Fortune—the tech mogul's bastard son."

She sucked in a breath. "Don't talk about Keaton like that. How do you even know about him?"

"I saw your mom yesterday," he answered with a shrug. "She agrees with me, Frannie. You're setting yourself up for a big fall with the Brit. I may not be perfect, but we come from the similar backgrounds. You and I fit together."

"You *cheated* on me," she said through clenched teeth. "I would never take you back, Lou. My mom knows that even if she pretends otherwise. Keaton is more of a man than you could ever hope to be. He—"

"Has a line of conquests in his wake longer than the line for the porta potties at a music festival." Lou moved toward her, pulling a folded piece of paper out of the inside pocket of his leather jacket. "I looked up your British Prince Charming and it appears he's bedded more women than James Bond. He may have a fancier accent, but he's going to break your heart just the same as me, Frannie."

"No," she whispered, unaware she'd spoken until Lou cocked a brow.

"See for yourself, sweetheart."

Her fingers automatically gripped the paper he shoved into them. Then he walked past her, calling over his shoulder, "You have my number when you come to your senses, Frannie. I won't wait forever."

He could wait until hell froze over for all she cared.

She didn't move from where she stood even after the door slammed shut and she was once again alone. Lou was a cheat and a liar. She should tear into shreds the paper he'd given her without even reading it.

Keaton *did* care about her. He was a decent man, and he'd never hurt her the way Lou had. The way her father had hurt her mother. The way his father...

The thought of Gerald Robinson—what he'd done to his family and the way that had shaped Keaton—prevented her from ripping apart the paper. After a few calming breaths, she opened the single sheet.

As she'd expected, it was the interview done by Ariana Lamonte, the blogger and reporter from *Weird Life Magazine*. What she hadn't expected was the focus on Keaton's dating history. The article wasn't defamatory, more like a puff piece on Keaton's legendary charm with flattering quotes from a half dozen of his previous girlfriends. Their comments ranged from veiled praise for his skill in the bedroom to the common theme that he was destined to be "the one that got away" for any woman lucky enough to date him.

The general consensus was now that Keaton had been recognized as part of the Fortune family, his popularity with the ladies would only grow.

Although Francesca was aware of his status as part of the Fortunes, and specifically the powerful Robinson branch of the family, it had been easy to ignore the differences in their lives as they'd spent time together over the past few weeks.

They'd both been raised by single mothers, which had felt like an important connection. Coupled with the way Keaton lavished attention on her and truly seemed to care more about who she was as a person than her station in life, Francesca had been able to ignore how very different they were. She realized now that she'd allowed herself to begin thinking about her relationship in the long term, making plans in her mind for when she finished school and where life would take them next. Together.

But he hadn't made her any promises or given the slightest indication that this was more than a passing diversion while he was working in Austin. He'd mentioned his half siblings but had never suggested Francesca meeting any of them and had been careful to schedule time spent with them away from Lola May's.

The more she thought about it, the more her mind raced and panic threatened to overtake her. The truth was Keaton had easily compartmentalized her place in his life. Other than when she'd shown up at the job site unannounced or meals at his apartment with just the two of them, she was no more a part of Keaton's world than she had been Lou's.

A choked sob escaped her mouth and she released

the paper, watching it flutter silently to the floor. Maybe she was overreacting. Please let her be over-reacting.

There was only one way to find out.

Chapter Thirteen

Keaton paused outside the mobile office onsite at Austin Commons. Once again, he could smell the intoxicating mix of vanilla and spice he would forever associate with Francesca.

Was his mind playing tricks on him or was he truly so enamored that her scent followed him wherever he went?

He took another deep breath and tipped up his head, the sun warm on his face even with the cool late January air. He smiled to himself as he opened the door to the office, thinking he was becoming too much of a Texan if fifty degrees in January felt cool. His mother had told him during a FaceTime chat last night that it had rained every afternoon the previous week, which was typical for late January in London.

"Have you read it?"

He jerked in surprise as he noticed Francesca sitting on the edge of one of the chairs at the small conference table in the office.

So the scent hadn't been a figment of his imagination. Even better.

"Hullo, luv," he said, not bothering to hide his grin as he mentally calculated how much time he'd have before one of his coworkers needed him and how soundproof the walls of the modular office were. "You gave me a fright but—"

Her lush mouth thinned. "Have you read it?"

Clearly Francesca wasn't in the same amorous mood as him, but Keaton had never shied away from a challenge. "If you could enlighten me as to the 'it' to which you refer," he told her as he loosened his tie, "I might be better equipped to answer your question." He arched a brow. "Also, would you mind very much taking off your clothes?"

She stood. "Because I'm a conquest to you?"

"No," he answered, holding out his hands, palms facing her. "I apologize, Francesca. After this week… our nights together…" He offered a small smile. "One would think I've had my fill, but my need for you seems more insatiable than my appetite for pie."

She didn't return his smile and a tremor of unease snaked through him. Had she tired of him so quickly? Was that even possible?

"I'm sorry," he said immediately. "What are you asking if I've read?"

"The blog." She seemed to answer the question without having to move her lips. Her mouth fascinated him, and it took a few seconds for his brain to register the word *blog*.

"The interview I did with Ariana?"

Francesca nodded.

"That's right. It was published today." He slipped into the chair behind the desk and pulled up his email. There was a message from Ariana with the URL for the blog post, and he clicked on it then turned his attention back to Francesca as the site loaded. "Was it horrible? Does it make me seem like a total prat?"

"You're a ladies' man," she whispered as if revealing some terrible secret.

"Ah, not exactly," he countered, even though he knew his reputation back in London as well as anyone. That part of his life seemed so far away from where he was now. Who he was in Austin and with Francesca. He glanced at the screen, which was taking its sweet time to load. "Is that what the interview—"

"It was flattering," Francesca clarified. "Ariana was obviously charmed. She's a good reporter. There were quotes from your ex-girlfriends, all of whom remain spellbound by you. You charm everyone—Lola May, Ciara…" She took shuddery breath, then added, "Me."

He pushed away from the desk, impatient with waiting. He could read the damned interview later. There was a note of accusation in Francesca's tone that seeped into his body like a poison, making his skin feel two sizes too small. "I'm getting the distinct impression that charming is bad."

She shook her head, but her eyes remained bleak. "Charming isn't bad but…is it real?"

The question irritated him and he felt the defenses he'd relied on for so many years spring to life. They'd gone dormant in response to his feelings for Francesca and the easy way she had of filling his heart. But now…

"What do you mean by *real*?" he asked cautiously.

"I wonder if your feelings for me are real," she answered, "or if what's between us is simply you being the winsome Brit who is always ready for a new challenge." As she squeezed her hands into fists, Keaton felt like his heart was locked in her grip. "I was the most recent conquest." His chest burned and ached, mainly because even though he wanted to deny her words, there was an underlying truth in them that wouldn't dissipate. "All of your ex-girlfriends seem to have one thing in common," she said. "They see you as the one who got away."

"I'm not—"

"Why haven't you settled down, Keaton?"

He shook his head. No one had ever questioned him or the choices he'd made in life. "The time has never been right," he said lamely. "My relationships have always been casual."

"To you," she countered. "Because you won't let them be any other way. What about us?"

He stood, ran a hand through his hair. It felt like the walls of the small office were closing in on him. "You know how I feel about you, Francesca."

"I don't," she murmured. "I know how I feel about you, Keaton." She took a step toward him then stopped when he instinctively shifted away. Pain flashed in her eyes, and he hated that he'd put it there. "I love you, Keaton." The words were soft but clear and they cut him open with the precision of a surgeon's blade. "I'm in love with you. I want to build a life with you. I want—"

"Don't." He closed his eyes as he struggled to keep a hold on the emotions tumbling through him. A piece of him had craved hearing those words from her. They were like a balm to his lonely soul, in the same way her effervescent sweetness had been these past few weeks.

But in the same way that champagne bubbles gave off an initial giddy fizz, like sparklers blazing in the dark then bursting on the tongue, he knew it couldn't last. He wasn't built for the kind of relationship Francesca wanted and deserved. Not as Gerald Robinson's—Jerome Fortune's—son. And just like too much champagne, overindulging in the fantasy of what he'd never be able to give would only lead to a wicked relationship hangover for both of them.

He could not—would not—hurt her that way.

"Why shouldn't I tell you how I feel?" Her beautiful brown eyes were sad, but she lifted her chin, as if daring him to deny her the right to her emotions. "I wasn't in this alone, Keaton. These past couple of weeks meant something."

"But not what you want them to mean," he said, forcing the words out past the regret clogging his throat. "You know my mother's history—how my father broke her heart. I can't—"

"You're not the same man he is," she insisted.

"We share the same blood. What if I become like him?" He held up a hand when she would have argued. "You're the one who called me a ladies' man. I like women, Francesca. I've dated plenty. I can't commit because I won't risk hurting someone the way my mother was hurt. If there are no promises, it can't end in heartache."

"Do you actually believe that?" She gave a harsh laugh and moved toward him, fire glinting in her gaze.

"You made a promise to me with each kiss, Keaton. Every touch was like a pledge. You may not have said the words, but I felt your love as clearly as if you'd written it across the sky. The fact that you can stand here and deny it…"

Her voice broke off and she drew in a shuddery breath. Her eyes remained dry but it was clear she was struggling to hold herself together. "I've known heartache, but this is something more. You are tearing me apart."

Her words practically split him in two. He hated hurting her and every fiber of his being screamed at him to rush forward, take her in his arms and tell her what she wanted to hear. But he stood still and forced his voice to be emotionless as he said, "I'm sorry."

She stared at him a moment longer, as if waiting for more. Waiting for something he wasn't able to give.

Finally she gave a shaky nod. "Then this is the end," she whispered.

"I'm sorry," he repeated. What else could he say?

Francesca walked out of the office and he stumbled back into the chair, his whole body numb. He read the blog, cringing slightly at the quotes from his ex-girlfriends. The piece was flattering, but Keaton hated the underlying truth of who he was contained in Ariana's words.

He might not be the adulterer his father was, but there was no doubt he was Gerald Robinson's son. The veracity of that fact was clear in the pain he'd caused Francesca with his inability to be the man she needed.

Despite all the childhood moments spent yearning for a father, Keaton wished he could ignore his connection to the man who'd broken his mother's heart.

He wished he'd done a better job of protecting the heart of the woman who meant so much to him.

The woman whose loss he felt like he'd carved out a piece of himself.

Through sheer force of will, Francesca held herself together during her afternoon shift at Lola May's. The diner was blessedly busy, so she had little time to contemplate the disastrous end to her relationship with Keaton as she hurried to serve her customers. But she absently rubbed at her chest as she put in an order, somewhat stupefied to find her body intact when it felt like all that was left of her heart was an empty, gaping hole.

Ciara gave her a sympathetic smile from across the restaurant. It was clear her roommate, as well as Lola May and several of the regular patrons who'd witnessed her budding romance with Keaton, could tell something had gone horribly wrong. Thankfully no one spoke of it of while she was working. Francesca had no intention of adding humiliation to heartbreak by crumpling to a weeping heap on the diner's scuffed floor.

She hoped to sneak out quietly after her shift. But as she hung up her apron later that evening, she turned to find Ciara blocking her path.

"Lola May wants to see you in her office," her friend said gently.

"Ci, I can't," Francesca whispered, her voice threatening to break.

"I'm not asking for details yet, but it's clear things are bad. You shouldn't be alone right now," Ciara insisted, "and I'm on until close."

Francesca bit down on her bottom lip and squeezed shut her eyes. As much as she didn't want to talk to anyone about what had happened with Keaton, delaying the inevitable wouldn't make it any easier. After a moment, she nodded. "I'll talk to her, but I want you know I'm going to be fine."

"Of course you are." Ciara gave her a quick hug. "We'll make sure of it."

Francesca refastened her messy ponytail and walked to the diner's small office.

"Have a seat, honey," Lola May said in her thick southern drawl, not taking her eyes off the computer screen.

"I'm fine, Lola May." Francesca repeated the words she'd said to Ciara minutes earlier as if the continuous refrain might make them true.

"The same way I was fine when my dirtbag husband took off for parts unknown."

Francesca slipped into the worn leather sofa against the far wall. "Keaton hasn't disappeared," she said.

"He didn't make his daily appearance at the diner." Lola May pushed her reading glasses onto the top of her head as she turned away from the computer.

"He's probably busy." Charming his next conquest, she thought in her mind and let out a tiny moan as a fresh round of pain stabbed at her heart.

"Does this have anything to do with your idiot of an ex-boyfriend daring to show his face here yesterday?" Lola May's blue gaze was sharp under the generously applied coat of mascara that was her trademark.

Francesca shrugged. "Lou paid me a visit, but I'm through with him. I learned my lesson the hard way with him."

"And Keaton?"

"Turns out," Francesca answered, "whatever was between us has run its course, as well." She couldn't stop the tears that spilled from her eyes and quickly swiped at her cheeks. "It was bound to end so it's probably a blessing that it happened now instead of later."

Lola May arched a brow. "Why is that?"

"Because now I only love him a little bit." Francesca clenched her fists so hard her nails dug into her palms. The small stab of pain was the only thing that allowed her to keep her voice steady. "Later it might be more and—"

"Oh, honey."

The tenderness in those two words broke the thin hold Francesca had on her emotions. She covered her face with her hands as sobs racked her. Lola May was at her side a moment later, enveloping her in a Shalimar-scented embrace.

"It's not tr-true," Francesca said when she could finally speak. "I don't love him a little, Lola May. I love him with everything I am."

"I know, darlin'," the diner owner crooned. "And you have one of the biggest hearts in all of the great state of Texas."

"How c-could I have let this happen again?" Francesca pressed closer to Lola May. "Why do I pick men who give me just enough emotional rope to hang myself? It's like I'm begging for the heart-break noose."

"Keaton is not cut from the same cheating cloth as Lou." Lola May's voice was sure.

"I thought I knew that, but then I read that article."

"The interview with the blogger from *Weird Life*?" Francesca straightened. "He's had so many girlfriends," she said miserably. "They all have fancy British names and there were even a couple of titles thrown in the mix. Each one was more beautiful than the next. Like I can compete with Lady Such and So English Rose."

Lola May smoothed her thumbs over the tracks of Francesca's tears. "You don't have to compete with anyone, and I never got the impression Keaton expected you to."

"I thought I was different." Francesca sniffed. "I thought I meant more to him, but he doesn't love me. I'm just a stupid girl who keeps kissing frogs and expecting them to turn into a prince. But that's not how life works."

"I don't know what spooked Keaton, but it was obvious to everyone with a working set of peepers that boy was crazy for you."

Francesca shook her head, still baffled by Keaton's callous brush-off. What was between them hadn't been a figment of her imagination. It was real. No matter how badly he'd hurt her, she would never give up her belief that it had been real. But that didn't change the fact that she was alone once again.

"I guess I just wasn't enough." That sentence felt like the tired, pathetic refrain of her life.

Lola May wrapped her in another tight hug. "You are more than enough, and any man who can't see that doesn't deserve you."

Chapter Fourteen

"I told you that fancy-pants Fortune would break your heart. Women like us aren't poised and polished enough for a man like that."

Francesca swallowed back a bitter laugh as her mother put a glass of sweet tea on the table in front of her. As sure as Lola May had sounded when she'd comforted Francesca last night, Paige was just as certain in her conviction.

"I didn't come here to talk about Keaton," Francesca said.

Her mother crossed her arms over her chest and leaned back against the kitchen counter. "It's obvious you're hurtin'. Your face is so red and blotchy it looks like you've been boo-hooing into your pillow all night long."

That wasn't exactly true, since sleep had eluded

Francesca for most of the night. She'd wound up on the couch in her apartment watching made-for-TV movies with Ciara at her side.

She ignored her mother's subtle jab and asked, "Why did you talk to Lou about Keaton and me?"

Paige's thin brows rose until they looked like they might become one with her hairline. "You have a history with Louis. He cares about you."

"Lou cares about himself," Francesca shot back, "and he always has."

"He's made mistakes, but he's truly sorry, Frannie. My instinct tells me he's changed."

Another laugh surged up in Francesca's throat. When it came to men, her mother had the instincts of a Kamikaze pilot hell-bent on his mission.

"Mom, I'm done with Lou."

"He understands who you are," her mother insisted. "And his band is really taking off, so he's going to need someone at his side to support him."

"Don't you mean wait on him hand and foot?"

Her mother sighed. "Frannie, sometimes love means making sacrifices."

"Not when what's being sacrificed is my self-respect."

"Do you think that Fortune is a better bet? With his highfalutin' accent and false promises?"

Francesca took a drink of tea then stood. "Keaton never promised me anything," she whispered, even though it felt like he had made a thousand promises to her heart. "But if he doesn't want me for who I am, he isn't a better bet. Maybe I have to believe I'm enough before I can expect anyone else to believe it." She moved forward and took her mom's hands. "We're both enough, Mom. Just the way we are."

Paige's eyes softened for a moment and Francesca could see the pain of a lifetime of disappointment in them. She didn't want that for herself. She wanted to live.

"Just the way we are," her mother whispered. "When did you get so wise, Frannie-girl?"

"I'm not wise yet," Francesca answered. "But I'm working on it."

"I do not belong here."

The following week, Keaton sat in the waiting area on the maternity floor of an Austin hospital where somewhere behind a set of swinging doors Ben's wife, Ella, was giving birth.

"Of course you do," his half sister Olivia told him sweetly as she paced back and forth. "If you weren't here, Sophie would be squeezing my fingers into oblivion and I value my bones too much for that sort of torture."

His youngest half sister, Sophie, flashed a sheepish smile and gentled the death-grip she had on his hand. She sat next to him in one of the dull gray upholstered chairs that lined the waiting room. "Sorry," she whispered. "I'm nervous."

"I don't mind," he told her and covered her small hand with his. "At least I can be of some use."

"Family doesn't have to be useful," Sophie said. "They just have to show up."

Family. Right, then.

Even if he wasn't ready to claim his father, the Fortune Robinson children were his family—his brothers and sisters.

"You have to say it," Olivia said, stopping in front of his chair.

Keaton felt his brows furrow. "Say what?"

"That you belong here with us."

"Very good. I appreciate you including me," he told her, flashing a smile. "Even if babies aren't my strong suit."

Her brown eyes narrowed. "Not good enough."

"Just say it," Sophie advised. "Once Olivia sets her mind to something, there's no use denying her."

Bloody hell. Three little words but they felt like some kind of pledge Keaton wasn't ready to make. "Wouldn't it be easier if we pricked our fingers and swore our fidelity to each other in blood?" he asked playfully, still trying to wield the charm that had been emphasized in the recent "Becoming a Fortune" profile.

"Say it," both sisters said at the same time.

Keaton swallowed and cleared his throat. So much for the charm. It hadn't done much to impress Francesca and clearly wasn't working on these two women.

"I belong here," he said finally.

Olivia beamed down at him while Sophie cheered.

Keaton couldn't help grinning in return. "Did you two always get your way?"

"Of course we always got our way. We had Rachel and Zoe then, too," Olivia answered, referring to their two sisters who had found and rediscovered love in the last two years. "We were a bit of a force."

"In our defense," Sophie added, "we had to put up with Ben, Wes, Kieran and Graham. Growing up with four brothers may have made some of us a little bossy."

Keaton thought about what it would have been like

to grow up in a big family. Who he would have become if he hadn't had the constant underlying need to prove himself to the father he never knew. Another wave of gratitude rushed through him for his mother and all she'd sacrificed. She'd been wounded deeply by Gerald Robinson but had never let it stop her from loving Keaton, even when he'd grown up to look so much like his father and brothers.

"Because we're now *your* pesky sisters," Olivia said, settling into the chair on his other side, "do you want to talk about what's wrong?"

"Er, what's wrong with what?"

"With you," Olivia said gently. "Ben told us about how happy you seemed the last time the two of you had lunch. He said it was because of a woman. But now you look like you've just lost your best friend."

Sophie nodded and this time the squeeze she gave his hand was more about comfort than her own panic. "We assume that has something to do with the same woman."

Keaton tugged at the collar of his crisp oxford-cloth shirt, which suddenly felt too tight.

Why had he wished for brothers and sisters again?

"You're stuck with us," Sophie said, as if reading his mind, "and unless Ben comes running through those doors to announce the birth of his baby, we're not letting you off the hook."

Keaton threw a longing glance at the door that led to the maternity ward, but Ben didn't miraculously emerge. "There was a woman," he admitted, "but I made a hash of it and now she's done with me. End of story."

"Nice try," Sophie said, giving his shoulder a nudge. "We want details."

"She's an Austin native," Keaton answered, the image of Francesca's beautiful smile filling his mind. "She waitresses in a diner near the job site where I've been working. She's also putting herself through school and is one of the hardest working, most determined people I've ever met. Her attitude never falters and she's not only gorgeous on the outside, but truly stunning on the inside. Every moment I spent with her was perfect. It didn't matter what we were doing— Francesca made every tiny aspect of life amazing." He let out a shaky laugh and looked between Sophie and Olivia, who were both staring at him like he was about to strip off his clothes and run naked through the hospital corridors.

"I was kind of talking about the details of how it ended," Sophie said quietly. "And now I'm even more confused because you clearly—"

"Love this Francesca," Olivia finished.

Keaton automatically shook his head. "That was the problem. I can't love her. I can't commit to a woman like that."

"Why?" Sophie demanded. "Do you have a wife hidden away in some decrepit English castle?"

"A decrepit castle?" Keaton asked, arching an eyebrow. "Someone is a fan of the Brontë sisters, I take it?"

"Ignore her," Olivia said. "She's too much of a romantic."

Sophie leaned forward and spoke across Keaton. "There's no such thing as too much of a romantic."

Olivia rolled her eyes. "Was it a small hash or a royal one?"

"Royal," Keaton confirmed. "She'd seen the blog interview Ariana Lamonte did and the bits from my ex-girlfriends made her nervous. She wanted to make sure that things were different between us. That I was different."

"And you?" Sophie prompted.

"Responded like the jackass I am." He shrugged. "I can't be different, and she can't love me. Even though I only recently discovered that I'm Gerald's son, I'm too much like him." He held up his hands when Olivia let out a gasp. "I would never cheat on her, but I'll hurt her just the same."

"It sounds like you already have," Sophie murmured.

Keaton blew out a breath through the vise that was slowing choking off his lungs. "I didn't mean it to end that way."

Sophie's delicate brows furrowed. "But you meant it to end?"

"It was bound to," he said and ran a hand through his hair. "I can't be the man she deserves."

"Because you don't care enough?" Olivia asked. "Or because you're a yellow-bellied coward?"

"I care," Keaton answered, even though that made him a coward in his sister's eyes. But he wasn't. He was a realist with strong self-preservation instincts. Nothing less and definitely nothing more.

"You aren't our father," Sophie told him, her tone achingly gentle. "I know it's difficult with what he's done and how he's behaved. Trust me, the fact that our family seems to be growing exponentially has not been easy for the eight of us. But you can't let that define you."

"It already has," Keaton answered, realizing that *coward* might be the perfect designation for him.

Olivia shook her head. "It doesn't have to anymore. Look at Ben, Wes and Graham. They found women who were worth risking their hearts to win and that's what they did. It's out there for you, Keaton. You'll find the right woman and—"

"He already has," Sophie interjected, popping up from her seat. "Now you need to fight for her. Make her love you." She spread her arms wide. "You need a *grand gesture.*"

Keaton couldn't help the smile that tugged up one corner of his mouth. "Is that so?"

"Don't listen to her," Olivia counseled. "We've already established that she's too romantic."

"That's not true." Sophie made a face at her sister. "Zoe made Joaquin fall in love with her and they're happy as two pigs in a poke. It is absolutely possible to make someone love you." She pointed to Keaton. "And he has an advantage. His Francesca already told him she loved him. Now he just has to force her to give him another chance."

His Francesca.

The thought of the beautiful, bubbly waitress belonging to him made Keaton's heart stumble to find purchase as his whole world seemed to shift and fall into place. Of course he loved her. Bloody hell, he'd loved her almost from the moment he saw her. He truly had been the worst sort of coward to let his doubts destroy his opportunity to find happiness with her.

"I'm not sure another chance is possible," Keaton said, shaking his head. "I've called and texted, trying to apologize. She won't return either. It's clear she's finished with me."

Sophie crouched low until they were at eye level and said slowly, "Grand. Gesture."

He opened his mouth to respond but just then the door to the maternity ward swung open and Ben came through. His face was lit with the most astounding mix of joy and relief Keaton had ever witnessed.

"She's here," he shouted as both of his sisters rushed forward. "Baby Lacey has made her grand entrance and she's perfect."

Sophie gave a happy squeal then asked, "How's Ella?"

"She made it through like a trooper." Ben's expression turned tender. "There are no words," he murmured, "for how strong and amazing my wife is. She's my hero."

Olivia hugged her brother. "Tell us about the baby. Who does she look like? Does she smell sweet like a baby?"

"Does she have hair?" Sophie demanded.

Ben chuckled and wrapped an arm around each of his sisters. "Come and see for yourself. Ella is settled in the room with the baby, and she sent me out to get you."

Sophie bounced up and down on her toes. "Let's go." She moved to where the sisters had left an enormous stack of boxes and gift bags on one of the waiting room's side tables. "Keaton, will you help me carry all of this?"

"I should give you time together," he said quickly, coming to his feet. "I'll stop back later and—"

Ben pointed a finger at him. "You are not leaving

me with four women. There's got to be something in the Bro Code about that."

"I'm not sure the Bro Code applies to newborn babies," Keaton said with a grimace. But he took the boxes and bags Sophie handed him and followed his siblings down the corridor.

A sharp pain stabbed through his chest the moment he saw Ella propped up in the hospital bed, a small bundle cradled in her arms. He'd never imagined himself as a family man. He didn't even particularly care for babies with their soggy nappies and blood-curdling cries.

But Ella, with her wavy auburn hair and bright blue eyes, looked so blissfully happy holding little Lacey. It was as if everything in her life had led to this perfect moment and the beginning of the family she and Ben had created. He couldn't help but wonder what Francesca would look like holding his baby. There was no doubt she'd be a wonderful mother, patient and sweet, making every day an adventure. He thought about how hard his mother had been forced to work to make a life for him, and he realized suddenly that he wasn't anything like his father.

Gerald Robinson had no problem leaving behind a trail of broken hearts and unwanted children. If Keaton became a father, he would give everything he had to being the best parent he could. He would make sure he knew their mother was loved and cherished for her entire life.

His head pounded at the sudden realization that he did not have to turn out like his father. He could choose to be a different man. A man who deserved to call Francesca his own.

His gaze caught Sophie's from across the bed where she and Olivia were huddle over baby Lacey. His little sister winked and mouthed, "Grand gesture."

Keaton gave a small nod, the wheels already turning in his brain.

Chapter Fifteen

Before Keaton could charge back into Francesca's life, slaying the dragons he had created, he needed to be certain he was doing the right thing. He left the hospital in the early afternoon and checked in at the office onsite at the Austin Commons before heading back to his apartment.

On the way he passed Lola May's, glancing up at the windows of the apartment above the diner. Was Francesca working or at class or was she in her apartment? What would happen if he charged back into her life right now? Was there any possibility she remained as consumed with thoughts of him as he was with her? When she'd walked away, it had felt as though she was well and truly finished with him. Despite Sophie's belief that it was possible to make a person fall in love—or in Keaton's case, fall back in love—he couldn't shake the image of Francesca as she turned away from him.

Enlightenment while surrounded with all the joy that went with greeting a newborn quickly faded in the lonely reality of returning to his empty apartment. Without the energy and gentle prodding of his sisters, Keaton's doubts reemerged, stronger than ever. He closed the black-out blinds and sat on the sofa in the darkened apartment. Only the glow from his thin laptop lit the room as he read and re-read the interview he'd done for the *Weird Life* blog.

Was he no more than the man his former girlfriends had described, attentive and kind but ultimately not mature enough to commit more than a few months of fun and laughs? The truth could be that he was truly broken on the inside, warped by the stigma of growing up without a father then learning that the man he'd always hoped to impress was less than honorable in his dealings with women.

Slamming shut the computer, he reached for the cell phone he'd tossed to the cushion next to him.

His mother picked up on the first ring. "Keaton, what a lovely surprise. Is everything all right?"

"Yes," he answered automatically, then took a breath and said, "No, Mum, it's not. I'm sorry to call so late." With the six-hour time difference, it was almost ten at night in London.

"You can call whenever you need me. I'll always be here."

"I know," he murmured.

"What is it, sweetheart? Did something happen with the Fortunes?"

"Ben's wife had the baby."

He heard his mother's startled gasp and quickly added, "Baby Lacey is absolutely perfect. I was waiting at the hospital with Sophie and Olivia so I had a chance to see her."

His mother laughed. "I can't imagine you on a maternity floor, Keaton. Babies were never really your strong suit. Did you hold her?"

"I did. Rather expertly I might add."

"America is changing you," his mother said. "For the better, I think."

"I'm not sure about that," he admitted, "which is why I'm calling. Tell me about your relationship with Gerald Robinson. I need to understand what drew you to him."

A charged silence filled the line. His mother had rarely spoken of the man who had utterly broken her heart. Even after Ben had tracked down Keaton last year in London and he'd discovered his connection to the Fortune family, Anita had remained resolutely silent on the subject.

"I was a different person back then," she said after a moment. "I was young and quite immature, a recent transplant to the city from Hampshire. Nothing could have prepared me for the energy of London. Everything seemed new and limitless, and I'm ashamed to admit I lost myself for a bit."

"Gerald Robinson took advantage of you," He didn't bother to hide the bitterness in his tone. To think of his mother as a wide-eyed country girl in the city, the perfect prey for someone like his father, made Keaton's blood boil.

"Maybe in hindsight," she admitted, almost reluctantly, "but I wanted him. He was a powerful force

and I was drawn to his charisma. He was like everything exciting and new about London all wrapped up
in one person." He heard her take a breath through the
phone. "We met at the office. I was a temporary re-
ceptionist, astounded that someone like Gerald would
even notice me. I think I fell for him the first moment
I saw him. There was nothing that would have stopped
me from being with him, Keaton. It was more than a
case of not looking before I leapt. I rushed headlong
off a cliff with no thought of a parachute or anything
to break my fall at the bottom."

"He should have been the one to catch you."

"That wasn't in his makeup," she whispered and
Keaton felt his chest tighten. That was exactly the kind
of innate callousness he feared he shared with his father. "We were only together a short time," his mother
continued, "and he never made me any promises."

Just like Keaton had never made promises to Francesca. His heart sank even further.

"It was only after I realized I was pregnant that I
discovered he had a wife back in the States. Not that
he tried to hide it necessarily, but I couldn't concep-
tualize that a man could lavish so much attention on
me while he was committed to another."

"I'm sorry, Mum." Keaton wished he'd never asked
the question now that the answers seemed to burn a
hole deep inside him.

"Don't be sorry," his mother said firmly. "I actually owe Gerald Robinson a debt of gratitude because
you were the result of my brief affair. You made everything worth it, Keaton."

"But he broke your heart," Keaton insisted. "He
broke...you."

"No, sweetie," she said, her voice thick with emotion. "He changed me and forced me to grow up sooner than I might have otherwise. In some ways, it made me stronger. Being your mother made me the person I am today."

Keaton sighed. Was this his mother protecting him in the gentle way she always had? He hated to push her, especially when he knew how difficult it must be for her to speak of that time. But he had to know the truth. His future with Francesca depended on it.

"You never dated. You never found love again. It kills me to know you've spent your life alone because of me and Gerald Robinson."

His mother laughed softly. "Keaton Alistair Whitfield, do you think you are privy to every nuance of my life? That a mother would confide the secrets of her dating life to her young son?"

"There were no secrets." He choked a little on the final word. "You had no dating life, Mum. I would have…known."

"It was my job to love and protect you." His mother's tone was mildly chiding. "You have always been the heart of my life, Keaton, but not the whole of it."

He felt his mouth drop open. "Do you mean—"

"I dated," Anita told him. "Nothing serious while you were a lad. Between taking care of you and my jobs, where would I have found the time or energy for—"

"Point taken," he interrupted quickly. God and the Queen save him from having a conversation with his mother about her sex life.

She chuckled again. "There were men. Mother was

my most important role but I never stopped being a woman. And now…"

Keaton gulped. "Now?"

"I've met someone lovely," his mother said, her voice taking on a girlish tone that was totally unfamiliar. "His name is Bertram Morgan. He lives around the corner and we take the same bus in the morning. His wife died a few years ago and his children have their own lives, like you do. We've been dating a few months so it was too new for me to mention to you." She paused then added, "But I'm in love, Keaton. After all these years, I've found my true love."

"Bloody hell," Keaton muttered.

"Language," his mother scolded. "I certainly hope that isn't the sum total of your reaction."

"Of course not. I'm happy for you, Mum," he said quickly. "You deserve…everything. This chap had better know how lucky he is to have you. If ever he—"

"He knows."

Right. Keaton was utterly astounded at this new twist in his reality. He'd always carried with him the heavy weight of knowing that his very existence had ruined his mother's chance for a happy life. To realize that she hadn't let Gerald Robinson's betrayal define her in the way it had Keaton made the foundation of his world shift again under his feet.

"I'm still your mother," Anita continued. "I want you to be happy, too. Love is a magical thing when you find the right person, Keaton. I have a feeling you are already well aware of that. From the moment you started talking about your Texas waitress, I knew she was special."

"You can't possibly understand *how* special," Keaton

murmured. "Francesca is the most amazing woman, Mum. And I've been an unmitigated arse."

"Keaton, no. I don't believe it. Women gravitate to you and they always have."

"I've never cared about any other woman like I do Francesca. I hurt her deeply. Have you ever heard of love making someone stupid?"

"All the time," his mother assured him. "The important question is how are you going to fix it?"

"I don't know if she'll trust me again."

"But you must try," Anita insisted. "You deserve to be happy."

He wasn't sure if he agreed but he knew he'd fight like hell to get another chance to be the kind of man Francesca deserved.

"A grand gesture," he muttered.

"What?"

"Sophie told me I need a grand gesture to show Francesca that I've changed. To win her back."

"Whatever it takes," his mother told him. "You're smart and creative. I'm sure you can come up with something special. But I'm guessing Francesca fell in love with your beautiful heart, my dear boy. The one you guard like the crown jewels in the Tower of London. Show her your heart, Keaton."

"Thanks, Mum," he said and they disconnected. The prospect of a grand gesture actually seemed less daunting than opening his heart. There was so much risk of having it broken.

He took comfort in knowing that his mother had not only survived her broken heart, as he'd assumed, but had become brave enough to give it to a good man.

Francesca had been brave in professing her love,

and he'd hurt her by spurning her declaration. He rubbed a hand along the back of his neck. He had such an enormous mistake to fix.

He stood and paced to the windows that looked out to the front of the building. An older couple was crossing the street and he watched as the man placed his hand on the small of the woman's back, guiding her off the curb with the unconscious tenderness that came from sharing decades of living with the same person. It wasn't a phenomenon Keaton had witnessed in his life, but he craved it nonetheless.

And there was only one woman he wanted at his side.

"Your shift was over an hour ago." Lola May gave Francesca's hip a gentle nudge. "Go home, honey."

Francesca moved to grab two plates from the pass through to the kitchen then slid them in front of the customers sitting at the diner's long counter. Ernie and Frank were regulars and had lunch together at the diner at least four days a week. Both in their late sixties, Ernie was divorced and Frank had never married. In many ways, they were like the Odd Couple, and she knew Lola May's had become a mainstay in their lives.

She ignored the dull ache in her gut at the thought that she could end up with Ciara and the diner as her only two constants and plastered a bright smile on her face. "Enjoy, fellas. Ernie, I'll grab your side of ranch for the fries."

The older man's craggy face split with a huge grin. "That's why I love you, Frannie. You know what I want before I even ask for it."

At least someone found her lovable, Francesca

mused as she opened the glass-fronted refrigerator where the condiments were stored. She could feel the weight of Lola May's gaze but did her best to avoid eye contact with her boss.

Since her breakup with Keaton last week, Francesca had been spending whatever free time she had at the diner. Even when Lola May's wasn't bustling with activity, there was always something to keep her busy. At the moment, they had enough filled ketchup bottles and stuffed napkin holders to make it through a zombie apocalypse. Anything was better than being alone. Ciara included her as much as she could, but Francesca couldn't keep up with her roommate's boisterous friends.

She placed the small plastic cup of ranch dressing on the counter, re-filled the ice tea for both men and then checked in with the other customers seated at the counter.

Turning to grab the pitcher of water on the back counter, she yelped a little when Lola May stepped into her space.

"Look at me, Francesca."

Francesca bit her lip but eventually raised her gaze.

"You don't want to stay here all day."

"You're wrong," she whispered. "I don't want to go upstairs to an empty apartment. Ciara is out with friends."

"Why don't you meet up with them?"

"I'm terrible company," Francesca answered. "Ciara has been inviting me to everything she does but I know it's a total downer for her friends. I don't have any big projects or exams on the horizon for school, so all I do is sit around and mope about Keaton. It's pathetic."

Lola May placed her hands on either of Francesca's

shoulders. "You are not pathetic—not by a long shot. You should call him back and see what he has to say."

Francesca shook her head. "What could he say that would make a difference? I love a man who doesn't love me back—story of my life. It would only hurt worse to hear his voice. Fool me once, shame on you. Fool me twice—"

"Holy crap, it's James Bond."

Ernie's gruff voice boomed through the diner and the whole place went silent.

Francesca gasped as her gaze darted to the front entrance and landed on Keaton, who stood in the doorway wearing a tuxedo that definitely looked worthy of 007 himself. Keaton was handsome as sin wearing a normal suit—or wearing nothing at all for that matter. But the combination of the tailored white shirt, fitted jacket and black bow tie made her mouth go dry even as her heart pounded a frantic rhythm against her rib cage.

He met her gaze, his blue eyes so darkly intense to look almost otherworldly. He didn't speak, but with a slight nod he began to walk—or more accurately prowl—toward her.

"Takes my breath away," Lola May muttered and moved to the far side of the counter.

Francesca had a fairly good idea of what an injured gazelle felt like when faced with a hungry lion. Keaton's gaze, an equal mix of sexy and intimidating, never wavered from hers.

The effect was so overwhelming that she forgot her broken heart, her anger at how he'd treated her and practically her own name.

Then she realized she was holding her breath and

gasped in a gulp of air just as he came toe-to-toe with her.

"Hullo, Francesca," he said softly.

Her name on his lips in that posh British accent had her knees threatening to give way. She managed a small nod and asked, "Do you have a date with the Queen?"

One side of his mouth quirked. "Only with the queen of my heart."

Francesca clasped a hand over her mouth as a giggle bubbled up in her throat.

"Too corny?" he asked.

She shook her head but actual speech seemed beyond her at the moment.

"It's perfect, darlin'," Lola May drawled from behind her. "Keep going."

Color burned on Francesca's cheeks as it dawned on her that the entire restaurant was focused on the scene playing out between Keaton and her. "Should we," she asked, clearing her throat, "go someplace more private to speak?"

"No, Francesca. I don't care who hears me. In fact..." His gaze swept the diner before settling back on her. "I want everyone to know how much I love you."

With a gasp, she took a step away from him. "Keaton," she whispered, "you don't have to say that."

"I do." He moved close again, crowding her space. She could feel the heat of his body, breathe in the scent of cologne that never failed to send butterflies dancing across her middle. "There are no words to tell you how sorry I am for hurting you, luv. But you must know that it was only me being a bloody fool."

As much as she wanted to believe him, her own doubts tumbled through her mind and heart. "I don't know that." She'd replayed his words a thousand times over in her head. "You seemed so sure and—"

"What I'm sure about," he said, cupping her cheeks between his palms, "is that you are the best damned thing that's ever happened to me."

There was a collective sigh from the diner's staff and customers, but Francesca couldn't take her eyes off Keaton. A sliver of hope glimmered in her heart, like the first ray of sun glinting through the clouds after a Texas rainstorm.

"I never imagined feeling about anyone the way I feel for you, sweetheart. Each morning when I wake up, you are the first thought I have, and at night, your laughter is the lullaby that sends me to sleep. Everything about you—the very essence of who you are—fascinates me. I could spend my whole life loving you and it still wouldn't be enough time to make you understand all the ways I adore you."

Francesca's heart stumbled in her chest. "Your whole life?"

"If you'll give me another chance." His thumbs were infinitely tender as they stroked back and forth across her cheeks. "Please, Francesca, give me the chance to prove that I can be the man to deserve your love."

"Yes," she whispered and the whole restaurant erupted with cheers and whistles.

Keaton kissed her with the kind of passion that turned her body to a quivering mass of desire. Then he was scooping her up and carrying her toward the door. She felt safe and right in the cradle of his arms, and she nuzzled her nose into the crook of his throat and breathed him in. Was it possible that this man—this Fortune—could truly be hers?

"I have one more question for you," he said as someone held open the door and they moved into the bright sunshine of the late January afternoon.

"What is it?"

He claimed her mouth for a kiss so exquisite it made all their other kisses seem like a prelude to this moment. Then her feet were on the ground, and if he hadn't pulled her tight against him, she might have melted into a puddle on the sidewalk.

"Look up," he told her.

"That's not a question," she answered, unable to resist teasing him. At the same time she registered the sound of an engine high above them. Her breath caught in her throat as she put a hand over her forehead to shade her eyes and looked up to where an airplane had scribed the words *Marry Me?* against the blue sky.

"Did you—"

"You told me you could feel my love as clearly as if was written across the sky. That's what I'm offering you, Francesca. My love and my life are yours if you'll have me." She felt him shift then gasped when he dropped to one knee. "Will you have me? Say you'll marry me and make me the happiest bloke on either side of the Atlantic."

He pulled out a black velvet box and opened it to reveal the most amazing diamond ring she'd ever seen. It had a brilliant center stone with a row of rubies on either side. "I know it's fast, but I swear my heart knew you were the one the first moment I walked into Lola May's and saw you."

She choked back a happy sob and whispered, "I think it was the pie."

"It was you," he said, his voice tender. "It will always be you."

"Oh, Keaton."

He made a face. "Can you clarify? Is that 'oh, Keaton,' yes, or 'oh, Keaton,' no? And please don't let it be 'no.' Please let me prove to you every day for the rest of our lives how much I love you."

She could see the love shining in his eyes, real and true and everything she'd ever dreamed about. But it was the slight hint of vulnerability that made the last of her doubts melt away. This man was written on her heart and she would spend forever loving him.

"Yes."

He slipped the ring on her finger then straightened and lifted her into his arms. She kissed him fiercely, laying her claim to his love.

When she finally glanced up, Keaton used one finger to turn her head back toward the restaurant. The large windows were filled with the diner's waitstaff and customers. Lola May was at the front, wiping tears from her cheeks.

"Francesca Fortune Whitfield," Keaton whispered. "It sounds perfect to my ears."

She beamed up at him. "As long as we're together, I'll take whatever life hands us, perfect or not."

"A perfectly imperfect love," he told her. "You and me forever."

Epilogue

"What if she doesn't like me?"

Keaton dropped a kiss on the tip of Francesca's nose then turned to the edge of the sidewalk and held out a hand to hail a taxi. "My mum's going to love you. They all will."

The streets around Trafalgar Square in central London were bustling, and he kept his fingers intertwined with Francesca's. He wasn't going to risk having her swept away in a tide of locals and tourists out on a rare sunny Saturday afternoon.

The truth was he'd had trouble letting Francesca out of his sight since she'd agreed to his proposal a week ago. It was still difficult to believe his beautiful waitress had given him a second chance. The first thing Keaton had done after introducing her to his half siblings was book two tickets for London. He couldn't wait for his mother to meet the woman he loved with his whole heart. Luckily, Francesca had a long weekend off from classes the first part of February and Lola May had been more than accommodating in switching her shifts.

They'd arrived in London just this morning for a whirlwind weekend. He'd assumed Francesca would be exhausted from taking the red-eye, but she'd been brimming with energy and had insisted on a tour of all of his favorite places in London. They'd managed to visit his flat, the British Museum and several shops in the Bloomsbury neighborhood, along with a tour of Harrods and a quick walk through Hyde Park before stopping to view the iconic stone lions in Trafalgar Square. Now they were headed to his mother's house to take tea with her and her girlfriends.

A black cab pulled up to the curb and Keaton held the door for Francesca, her blond curls whipping in the brisk winter wind. She pulled down her knit cap as she entered the cab then snuggled close to him when he slid in next to her.

"How did you live through London winters growing up?" she asked for the umpteenth time that day. "I can't believe how cold it is here."

"It's actually warmer than normal thanks to the sunshine. When the weather is gray and misty, the chill seeps into your bones." He wrapped an arm around Francesca's shoulder as he gave the driver directions to his mother's home. "But if cold weather means you'll cuddle up to me," he said, pressing a kiss to her rosy cheek, "I think we'll be planning an Antarctic honeymoon."

She shivered and wound her hands under his coat and around his waist. "At the beach, I'll cuddle *and* wear a bikini," she told him, her teeth chattering a little as she spoke.

"The beach it is," he agreed, his mouth going dry at the thought of Francesca in a two-piece bathing suit.

They hadn't begun to discuss wedding plans, and for now Keaton was content to enjoy the fact that Francesca belonged to him. But he wasn't going to wait too long. The amount of satisfaction he derived from the thought of joining his life with hers still shocked him, especially after all of the doubts he'd harbored. But as his mother had told him, love could be a magical thing with the right person.

"You have to promise to cut me off if I start babbling to your mom and her friends," she said.

He shook his head. "I love hearing you talk."

Francesca let out a little groan. "I'm so nervous I'll probably spill a cup of tea in her lap."

"There's no reason to be nervous, luv. All my mum has ever wanted is for me to be happy. You make me happy."

She nuzzled her nose against his throat, and Keaton sucked in a breath. "Bloody hell, your nose is as frigid as an ice cube."

"I'm a native Texan. I wasn't made for cold weather." She pressed closer. "I swear I don't think I'll ever warm up."

"Leave that to me," he said and trailed hot, openmouthed kisses along the underside of her jaw.

"Keaton, we're in a taxi."

He nipped at her sensitive earlobe. "I'd venture to guess the driver has seen worse."

With a laugh, she pushed him away. "Save that for later."

"Later," he agreed and the thought of feasting on Francesca spread out across the sheets of his huge bed had him stifling a groan.

It was a short ride to the Clapham neighborhood where his mother lived in south London. He pointed out various landmarks and styles of architecture along the way, hoping his incessant talking would distract her.

As soon as the cab pulled up in front of the modest redbrick row house, his mum was out the front door and heading for the sidewalk. Keaton paid the driver then climbed out and swept his mother into a tight hug, her lavender scent enveloping him.

"Mum, I'd like you to meet—"

"The girl who is finally going to give Anita the grandbabies she so desperately wants," Lydia called from the front porch.

Keaton rolled his eyes at the comment from his mum's outspoken friend. "This is Francesca Harriman."

"It's so nice to meet you, ma'am," Francesca said and for a moment Keaton wondered if she was going to curtsy to his mother.

"I'm so happy Keaton found you." Anita took both of Francesca's hands in hers. "You're as beautiful as he's told me."

A brilliant smile lit Francesca's face as she reached out and wrapped her arms around Anita.

"Oh, my," his mother murmured. Londoners weren't typically known for their effusive greetings.

"Thank you for raising such an amazing man," Francesca said softly and Keaton heard his mother sniff.

"It was my great pleasure," she answered. "Let's

get you out of the cold. I can feel you shivering under your jacket."

"A spot of tea," Mary Jane called from where she stood next to Lydia and Jessa, "will warm the poor girl right up."

Keaton smiled as his mother linked arms with Francesca and led her up the cobblestone walk. The women fussed and clucked over Francesca, as enchanted with her Texas accent as the people in Austin had been by Keaton's London accent when he'd first arrived in America. They were also charmed by the fact that Francesca had brought small gifts for each of them from Austin.

She quickly relaxed and no tea was spilled during the visit. Instead there was much laughter as each of the women shared embarrassing stories of Keaton as a boy.

"She's lovely," Anita told him as he helped her refill the tray of pastries in the kitchen. As it turned out, his gorgeous Texan had a taste for the very British combination of scones and Devonshire cream.

"I'm glad you like her," he said and nipped a bite of a biscuit from the tray.

His mother gently slapped at his hand. "There's a lightness to you now, Keaton. You were always so determined and driven, but you relax with Francesca."

"She's good for me."

"As is America?"

He understood the question his mother was really asking. "England will always be home," he answered, "but I've found my place in Austin."

Anita studied him for a moment then nodded. "Francesca is your home."

"Yes."

"Then I suppose it's time I renew my passport," his mother told him. "Phone calls and FaceTime are all well and good, but I want to see this life you've built with my own eyes."

He let out a relieved breath, as the thought of telling his mother that he planned to stay in Texas had been weighing on him. "When do I get to meet your Bertram?" he asked.

"Tomorrow is his day off. Perhaps we could all have breakfast?"

"Very good." He picked up the tray once she'd placed the last scone on it. "I can tell he makes you happy, Mum. That makes me happy, as well."

"We'd better rescue Francesca before Lydia and Mary Jane frighten her away. They've already picked out names for your children, you know."

Keaton groaned and followed his mother back into the sitting room, a sense of contentment surrounding him as he watched the women who had raised him make Francesca a part of their tight circle. By the time they said goodbye to his mother and her friends almost two hours later, Francesca's eyelids were drooping.

"It's a food coma," she said as she rested her head on his shoulder in the black cab taking them back to his flat. "I ate my weight in clotted cream."

"It's also a perfect excuse for me to take you to bed," he said and that's exactly what he did.

They spent the rest of the day holed up in his flat, and Keaton had never been more thankful for the oversize shower he'd had installed as well as the luxury silk sheets that covered his bed.

"England is much warmer this way," Francesca said hours later as he curled her curvy body against his.

"I'm rethinking Antarctica," he told her. "I plan to spend the whole of our honeymoon wrapped around you, luv."

"Wherever we end up," she said, kissing him deeply, "it will perfect because we're together."

"Always and forever," he said and claimed her once again.

* * * * *

Don't miss the next installment of the new Harlequin Special Edition continuity

THE FORTUNES OF TEXAS: THE SECRET FORTUNES

Sophie Fortune Robinson is a starry-eyed romantic who believes she's found her Mr. Right. Little does she know that her real One True Love is right in front of her—the coworker who is determined to make her Valentine's Day a holiday to remember!

Look for
HER SWEETEST FORTUNE
by
USA TODAY *bestselling author Stella Bagwell*

On sale February 2016, wherever Harlequin books and ebooks are sold.

Can't get enough romance? Keep reading for a special preview of WILD HORSE SPRINGS, the latest engrossing novel in the RANSOM CANYON *series by* New York Times *bestselling author Jodi Thomas, coming in February 2017 from HQN Books!*

CODY WINSLOW THUNDERED through the night on a half-wild horse that loved to run. The moon followed them, dancing along the edge of the canyon as they darted over winter buffalo grass that was stiff with frost.

The former Texas Ranger watched the dark outline of the earth where the land cracked open wide enough for a river to run at its base.

The canyon's edge seemed to snake closer, as if it were moving, crawling over the flat plains, daring Cody to challenge death. One missed step might take him and the horse over the rim and into the black hole. They'd tumble maybe a hundred feet down, barreling over jagged rocks and frozen juniper branches as sharp as spears. No horse or man would survive.

Only, tonight Cody wasn't worried. He needed to ride, to run, to feel adrenaline pumping in his veins, to know he was alive. He rode hoping to outrun his dark mood. The demons that were always in his mind were chasing him tonight. Daring him. Betting him to take one more risk…the one that would finally kill him.

"Run," he shouted to the midnight mare. Nothing would catch him here. Not on his land. Not over land his ancestors had hunted on for thousands of years. Fought over. Died for and bled into. Apache blood, settler blood, Comanchero blood mixed in him as it did in this part of Texas. His family tree was a tumbleweed of every kind of tribe that ever crossed the plains.

If the horse fell and they went to their deaths, no one would find them for weeks on this far corner of his ranch. Even the canyon that snaked off the great Palo Duro had no name here. It wasn't beautiful like Ransom Canyon, with layers of earth revealed in a rainbow of colors. Here the rocks were jagged, shooting out of the deep earthen walls from twenty feet in some places, almost like a thin shelf.

The petrified-wood formations along the floor of the canyon reminded Cody of snipers waiting, unseen but deadly. Cody felt numb, already dead inside, as he raced across a place with no name on a horse he called Midnight.

The horse's hooves tapped suddenly over a low place where water ran off the flat land and into the canyon. Frozen now. Silent. Deadly black ice. For a moment the tapping matched Cody's heartbeat, then both horse and rider seemed to realize the danger at once.

Cody leaned back, pulling the reins, hoping to stop the animal in time, but the horse reared in panic. Dancing on her hind legs for a moment before twisting violently and bucking Cody off.

As Cody flew through the night air, he almost smiled. The battle he'd been fighting since he was shot and left for dead on the border three years ago was about to end here on his own land. The voices of all the ancestors who came before him whispered in the wind, as if calling him.

When he hit the frozen ground so hard it knocked

the air from his lungs, he knew death wouldn't come easy tonight. Though he'd welcome the silence, Cody knew he'd fight to the end. He came from generations of fighters. He was the last of his line, and here in the dark he'd make his stand. Too far away to call for help. And too stubborn to ask anyway.

As he fought to breathe, his body slid over a tiny river of frozen rain and into the black canyon.

He twisted, struggling to stop, but all he managed to do was tumble down. Branches whipped against him, and rocks punched his ribs with the force of a prizefighter's blow. And still he rolled. Over and over. Ice on his skin, warm blood dripping into his eyes. He tried bracing for the hits that came when he landed for a moment before his body rolled again. He grabbed for a rock or a branch to hold on to, but his leather gloves couldn't get a grip on the ice.

He wasn't sure if he managed to relax or pass out, but when he landed on a flat rock near the bottom of the canyon, total blackness surrounded him and the few stars above offered no light. For a while he lay still, aware that he was breathing. A good sign. He hurt all over. More proof he was alive.

He'd been near death before. He knew that sometimes the body turned off the pain. Slowly, he mentally took inventory. There were parts that hurt like hell. Others he couldn't feel at all.

Cody swore as loud as he could and smiled. At least he had his voice. Not that anyone would hear him in the canyon. Maybe his brain was mush; he obviously had a head wound. The blood kept dripping into his eyes. His left leg throbbed with each heartbeat and he couldn't draw a deep breath. He swore again.

He tried to move and pain skyrocketed, forcing him to concentrate to stop shaking. Fire shot up his leg and flowed straight to his heart. Cody took shallow breaths and tried to reason. He had to control his breathing. He had to stay awake or he'd freeze. He had to keep fighting. Survival was bone and blood to his nature.

The memory of his night in the mud near the Rio Grande came back as if it had been only a day ago, not three years. He'd been bleeding then, hurt, alone. Four rangers had stood on the bank at dusk. He'd seen the other three crumple when bullets fell like rain.

Only, it had been hot that night, so silent after all the gunfire. Cody had known that every ranger in the area would be looking for him at first light; he had to make it to dawn first. Stay alive. They'd find him.

But not this time.

No one would look for him tonight or tomorrow. No one would even notice he was gone. He'd made sure of that. He'd left all his friends back in Austin after the shooting. He'd broken up with his girlfriend, who'd said she couldn't deal with hospitals. When he came back to his family's land, he didn't bother to call any of his old friends. He'd grown accustomed to the solitude. He'd needed it to heal not just the wounds outside, but the ones deep inside.

Cody swore again.

The pain won out for a moment and his mind drifted. At the corners of his consciousness, he knew he needed to move, stop the bleeding, try not to freeze, but he'd become an expert at drifting that night on the border. Even when a rifle had poked into his chest as one of the drug runners tested to see if he was alive, Cody hadn't reacted.

If he had, another bullet would have gone into his body, which was already riddled with lead.

Cody recited the words he'd once had to scrub off the walls in grade school. Mrs. Presley had kept repeating as he worked, *Cody Winslow, you'll die cussing if you don't learn better.*

Turned out she might be right. Even with his eyes almost closed, the stars grew brighter and circled around him like drunken fireflies. If this was death's door, he planned to go through yelling.

The stars drew closer. Their light bounced off the black canyon walls as if they were sparks of echoes.

He stopped swearing as the lights began to talk.

"He's dead," one high, bossy voice said. "Look how shiny the blood is."

Tiny beams of light found his face, blinding him to all else.

A squeaky sound added, "I'm going to throw up. I can't look at blood."

"No, he's not dead," another argued. "His hand is twitching and if you throw up, Marjorie Martin, I'll tell Miss Adams."

All at once the lights were bouncing around him, high voices talking over each other.

"Yes, he is dead."

"Stop saying that."

"You stop saying anything."

"I'm going to throw up."

Cody opened his eyes. The lights were circling around him like a war party.

"See, I told you so."

One beam of light came closer, blinding him for a moment, and he blinked.

"He's hurt. I can see blood bubbling out of him in several spots." The bossy voice added, "Don't touch it, Marjorie. People bleeding have germs."

The gang of lights streamed along his body as if trying to torture him or drive him mad as the world kept changing from black to bright. It occurred to him that maybe he was being abducted by aliens, but he doubted the beings coming to conquer the world would land here in West Texas or that they'd sound like little girls.

"Hell," he said and to his surprise the shadows all jumped back.

After a few seconds he made out the outline of what might be a little girl, or maybe ET.

"You shouldn't cuss, mister. We heard you way back in the canyon yelling out words I've seen written but never knew how to pronounce."

"Glad I could help with your education, kid. Any chance you have a cell phone or a leader?"

"We're not allowed to carry cell phones. It interferes with our communicating with nature." She shone her flashlight in his eyes. "Don't call me *kid*. Miss Adams says you should address people by their names. It's more polite. My name is Melanie Miller and I could read before I started kindergarten."

Cody mumbled a few words, deciding he was in hell already and, who knew, all the helpers' names started with *M*.

All at once the lights went jittery again and every one of the six little girls seemed to be talking at the same time.

One thought he was too bloody to live. One suggested they should cover him with their coats; another voted for undressing him. Two said they would never touch blood. One wanted to put a tourniquet around his neck.

Cody was starting to hope death might come faster when another shadow carrying a lantern moved into the mix. "Move back, girls. This man is hurt."

He couldn't see more than an outline, but the new arrival was definitely not a little girl. Tall, nicely shaped, hiking boots, a backpack on her back.

Closing his eyes and ignoring the little girls' constant questions, he listened as a calm voice used her cell to call for help. She had the location down to latitude and longitude and described a van parked in an open field about a hundred yards from her location where they could land a helicopter. When she hung up, she knelt at his side and shifted the backpack off her shoulder.

As she began to check his injuries, her voice calmly gave instructions. "Go back to the van, girls. Two at a time, take turns flashing your lights at the sky toward the North Star. The rest of you get under the blankets and stay warm. When you hear the chopper arrive, you can watch from the windows, but stay in the van.

"McKenna, you're in charge. I'll be back as soon as they come."

Another *M*, Cody thought, but didn't bother to ask.

To his surprise the gang of ponytails marched off like tiny little soldiers.

"How'd you find me?" Cody asked the first of a dozen questions bouncing around in his aching head as the woman laid out supplies from her pack.

"Your cussing echoed off the canyon wall for twenty miles." Her hands moved along his body, not in a caress, but to a man who hadn't felt a woman's touch in years, it wasn't far from it.

"Want to give me your name? Know what day it is? What year? Where you are?"

"I don't have brain damage," he snapped, then regretted moving his head. "My name's Winslow. I don't care what day it is or what year for that matter." He couldn't make out her face. "I'm on my own land. Or at least I was when my horse threw me."

She might have been pretty if she wasn't glaring at him. The lantern light offered that flashlight-to-the-chin kind of glow.

"Where does it hurt?" She kept her voice low, but she didn't sound friendly. "As soon as I pass you to the medics, I'll start looking for your horse. The animal might be out here, too, hurting or dead. Did he fall with you?"

Great! His Good Samaritan was worried more about the horse than him. "I don't know. I don't think so. When I fell off the edge of the canyon, Midnight was still standing, probably laughing at me." He took a breath as the woman moved to his legs. "I tumbled for what seemed like miles. It hurts all over."

"How did this happen?"

"The horse got spooked when we hit a patch of ice," he snapped again, tired of talking, needing all his strength to handle the pain. Cusswords flowed out with each breath. Not at her, but at his bad luck.

She ignored them as she brushed over the left leg of his jeans already stained dark with blood. He tried to keep from screaming. He fought her hand as she searched, examining, and he knew he couldn't take much more without passing out.

"Easy," she whispered as her blood-warmed fingers cupped his face. "Easy, cowboy. You've got a bad break. I have to do what I can to stabilize you and slow the blood flow. They'll be here soon. You've got to let me wrap a few of these wounds so you don't bleed out."

He nodded once, knowing she was right.

In the glow of a lantern she worked, making a tourniquet out of his belt, carefully wrapping his leg, then his head wound.

Her voice finally came low, sexy maybe if it were a different time, a different place. "It looks bad, but I don't see any chunks of brain poking out anywhere."

He didn't know if she was trying to be funny or just stating a fact. He didn't bother to laugh. She put a bandage on the gash along his throat. It wasn't deep, but it dripped a steady stream of blood.

As she wrapped the bandage, her breasts brushed against his cheek, distracting him. If this was her idea of doctoring a patient with no painkillers, it was working. For a few seconds there, he almost forgot to hurt.

"I don't have water to clean the wounds, but the dressing should keep anything else from getting in."

Cody began to calm. The pain was still there, but the demons in the corners of his mind were silent. Watching her move in the shadows relaxed him.

"Cody," he finally said. "My first name is Cody."

She smiled then for just a second.

"You a nurse?" he asked.

"No. I'm a park ranger. If you've no objection, I'd like to examine your chest next."

Cody didn't move as she unzipped his jacket. "I used to be a ranger, but I never stepped foot in a park."

He could feel her unbuttoning his shirt. Her hand moved in, gently gliding across his ribs.

When he gasped for air, she hesitated, then whispered, "One broken rib." A moment later she added, "Two."

He forced slow, long breaths as he felt the cold night air pressing against his bare chest. Her hand crossed over his bruised skin, stopping at the scars he'd collected that night at the Rio Grande.

She lifted the light. "Bullet wounds?" she questioned more to herself than him. "You've been hurt bad before."

"Yeah," he said as he took back control of his mind and made light of a gunfight that almost ended his life. "I was fighting outlaws along the Rio Grande. I swear it seemed like that night almost two hundred years ago. Back when Captain Hays ordered his men to cross the river with guns blazing. We went across just like that, only chasing drug runners and not cattle rustlers like they did back then. But we were breaking the law not to cross just the same."

He closed his eyes and saw his three friends. They'd gone through training together and were as close as brothers. They wanted to fight for right. They thought they were invincible that night on the border, just like Captain Hays's men must have believed.

Only, those rangers had won the battle. They'd all returned to Texas. Cody had carried his best friend back across the water that night three years ago, but Hobbs hadn't made it. He'd died in the mud a few feet from Cody. Fletcher took two bullets but helped Gomez back across. Both men died.

"I've heard of that story about the famous Captain

Hays." She brought him back from a battle that had haunted him every night for three years. "Legend is that not one ranger died that night. They rode across the Rio screaming and firing. The bandits thought there were a hundred of them coming. But, cowboy, if you rode with Hays, that'd make you a ghost tonight and you feel like flesh and blood to me. Today's rangers are not allowed to cross."

Her hand was moving over his chest lightly, caressing now, calming him, letting him know that she was near. He relaxed and wished they were somewhere warm.

"You're going to make it, Winslow. I have a feeling you're too tough to die easy."

Don't miss WILD HORSE SPRINGS by
New York Times *bestselling author Jodi Thomas,*
available February 2017 wherever
HQN books and ebooks are sold!
www.Harlequin.com

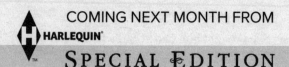
Available January 17, 2017

#2527 HER SWEETEST FORTUNE
The Fortunes of Texas: The Secret Fortunes • by Stella Bagwell
Sophie Fortune Robinson is certain the office heartthrob is her one true love, but when he turns out to be a dud, her friend Mason Montgomery is there to cheer her up. As they spend more time together, will they be able to set aside their insecurities to build a future together?

#2528 HIS PREGNANT COURTHOUSE BRIDE
Conard County: The Next Generation • by Rachel Lee
An unexpected pregnancy has high-class lawyer Amber Towers heading for Conard County—and Judge Wyatt Carter. Neither of them expected their law-school attraction to still be this strong, but their fledgling feelings have to weather Amber's wariness when it comes to love, not to mention nasty rumors and an election season, if they want to make it to a courthouse wedding.

#2529 BABY TALK & WEDDING BELLS
Those Engaging Garretts! • by Brenda Harlen
Widowed single dad Braden Garrett is looking for a mother for his adopted daughter, Saige, and librarian Cassie MacKinnon is the perfect candidate! But Cassie wants more than just a family—she wants a fairy-tale love to go along with it, and Brad's not sure he'll ever be the man able to give it to her.

#2530 THE COOK'S SECRET INGREDIENT
Hurley's Homestyle Kitchen • by Meg Maxwell
PI and single dad Carson Ford knows the fortune-teller who promised his dad a second great love was a fraud. He just needs the fortune-teller's daughter, Olivia Hurley, to explain that to his father. But the mystery woman sounds very much like her estranged aunt, so they set out to find her and just might find love for themselves along the way.

#2531 FALLING FOR THE REBOUND BRIDE
Wed in the West • by Karen Templeton
When Emily Weber flees a broken engagement, she never expected to meet her preteen crush in a New Mexico airport. But Colin Talbot is back and their attraction is undeniable, despite the trauma he experienced while traveling as a photographer. The timing couldn't be worse for a new relationship, but when fate goes to that much trouble, maybe they should listen...

#2532 HOW TO STEAL THE LAWMAN'S HEART
Sweet Briar Sweethearts • by Kathy Douglass
Widowed chief of police Trent Knight never expected Carmen Shields, the woman he blames for his wife's death, to be the one to make him love again. Yet Carmen is not only finding her way into his daughters' affections, she seems to be stealing his heart, too.

YOU CAN FIND MORE INFORMATION ON UPCOMING HARLEQUIN® TITLES, FREE EXCERPTS AND MORE AT WWW.HARLEQUIN.COM.

HSECNM0117

Wrapped more tightly in the shawl, she clomped across
the wooden porch, the sound then muffled in the dirt
as she made her way past the paddock to the foreman's
cabin. The clear, starry night was silent and still, save
for the thrum of crickets' chirping, the distant howl of
a coyote. The cabin's front door swung open before she
reached Colin's porch, a spear of light guiding her way.
And with that, the full ramifications of what she was
doing—or about to do, anyway—slammed into her.

But she had no idea what it might mean to Colin,
she thought as his broad-shouldered silhouette filled the
doorway, fragmenting the light. Maybe nothing, really—
oh, hell, her heart was about to pound right out of her
chest—since men were much more adept at these things
than women. Weren't they?

Spudsy scampered out onto the porch from behind
Colin's feet, wriggling up a storm when he saw her,
and Emily's heart stopped its whomping long enough to

squeeze at the sight of the bundle of furry joy she'd come to love.

At least she'd be able to keep the dog, she thought as she scooped up the little puppy to bury her face in his ruff, trying to ignore Colin's piercing gaze.

Oh, hell. That whole "sex as fun" thing? Who was she kidding? That wasn't her. Never had been. What on earth had made her think a single event would change *her*?

Although this one just might.

"I made a fire," Colin said quietly. Carefully. As though afraid she might spook. Never mind this had been her idea.

"That's nice."

Ergh.

Something like a smile ghosted around his mouth. "We can always just talk. No expectations. Isn't that what you said?" He shoved his hands into his pockets. "You're safe, honey. With me." His lips curved. "*From* me."

Still cuddling the puppy, she came up onto the porch. Closer. Too close. But not so close that she couldn't, if she were so inclined, still grab common sense by the hand and run like hell.

"And from myself?"

"That, I can't help you with."

Another step closer. Then another, each one a little farther away from common sense, whimpering in the dust behind her. "Kiss me," she whispered.

Don't miss
FALLING FOR THE REBOUND BRIDE
by Karen Templeton,
available February 2017 wherever
Harlequin® Special Edition books and ebooks are sold.

www.Harlequin.com

Turn your love of reading into
rewards you'll love with
Harlequin My Rewards

**Join for FREE today at
www.HarlequinMyRewards.com**

Earn **FREE BOOKS** of your choice.

Experience **EXCLUSIVE OFFERS** and contests.

Enjoy **BOOK RECOMMENDATIONS**
selected just for you.

PLUS! Sign up now
and get **500** points
right away!

Earn
FREE
REWARDS
Join
Today!
HarlequinMyRewards.com

MYR16R

THE WORLD IS BETTER WITH

Romance

Harlequin has everything from contemporary, passionate and heartwarming to suspenseful and inspirational stories.

Whatever your mood, we have a romance just for you!

Connect with us to find your next great read, special offers and more.

f /HarlequinBooks

🐦 @HarlequinBooks

www.HarlequinBlog.com

www.Harlequin.com/Newsletters

HARLEQUIN®

A *Romance* FOR EVERY MOOD™

www.Harlequin.com

SERIESHALOAD2015